CW01081936

WHAT NOW?

An anthology of Beckinsale's short stories

Amy C Beckinsale
©AmyCBeckinsale2022

Merry Christmas!

Love

Amy Bec ♡

8/11/22

SBN: 9798803314226
Imprint: Independently published

Cover design by: Art Painter
Library of Congress Control Number:
2018675309
Printed in the United States of America

Introduction

I began writing almost six years ago, working on my debut novel, One Night Forever. When it was released, May 4th 2020, I discovered the world of the 'Writing Community' on Twitter, Facebook and Instagram and the friendships I gained were incredible! From the groups I joined, I was soon invited to be part of box sets, sharing pages with my new friends and fellow authors I admire and look up too. Collections that would make you laugh, cry and relate to, and I am proud to now have these stories in a collection of my own for readers to enjoy.
Amy ;)

Dedication

For Hubby G, and our feathered lovable parrot, Buddy.

Thank you AJ Mullican for assisting me with the paperback :)

MIRACLE AT MIDNIGHT
Amy C.Beckinsale

Ethan

"Chestnuts roasting on an open fire, Jack Frost nipping at my nose. Love's gone and left me all alone. How I'll go on, no one knows."

"Christ almighty Ethan. Ruin a classic, why don't you."

Levi, my mate. Always the realist. Doesn't hold back. But then again, I probably need to hear it. Hey! I'm Ethan. Recently dumped by the love of my life, four weeks before Christmas and honestly, I have never felt more alone in my life. Carrie. Just saying her name fills me with joy, love and then BOOM. Pain and heartbreak. I suppose I should tell you before we get too close. I was planning on asking her to marry me on Christmas Eve. Cliche, I know, but what else was there that I could give her I hadn't before? I had spoiled her rotten over the two years we'd spent together. Getting engaged felt like the next step. She, however, seemed to have other plans. Plans that included cutting me out of her life and burning all hope of mending any bridges. Now, instead of playing festive music, drawing the crowds in who will eventually try to steal my microphone at some inappropriate moment during a song, making me miss the keys of my piano, I've become the Scrooge of the festive season. And this time it was Nat King Cole, who was at the brunt of my dumped heart.

"She's not coming back Ethan, so can we please give it a rest?" Levi asked again for the millionth time. "You're bumming me out."

"When she comes back, then I'll stop." I lied. "Until then you've got these improved versions."

"Improved?" Levi said, leaning on the closed lid of the grand piano. "Hardly say that, mate. I'd call it ruining your career if the boss hears you moaning about Carrie breaking up with you again."

I cringed, hearing her name.

"I have two words for you. Move on."

"Says the guy who's last break up landed him a 'I'm not showering for a week and stinking out the flat'."

Yeah, Levi's trying to give me relationship advice when he spent a week in the flat, refusing to shower, eating pizza and playing video games. The guy's body odour literally felt like it was invading my nostrils!

"Hey, at least I kept my wallowing inside the privacy of my room?"

"Levi, you stank the flat out. It's seeped through your bedroom door and into the rest of the flat. Do you know how much aftershave and Lynx deodorant I had to use just walking through the hallway before work?" He rolled his eyes. He's actually denying he stunk the flat out. "Hands down, mate, you were disgusting!"

"At least I'm not on the verge of being fired."

Our boss, Mike, stood with his arms folded, watching our discussion on the stage. Shit. He knew. I'm screwed.

"Williams!" He yelled.

The dude's voice grated on my ears. High pitched. Like when the teacher used to scrap their nails down the blackboard to silence the class.

"Tell me you are not feeling sorry for yourself again? If I have to hear about that woman once more, instead of hearing you play the music I pay you for, I can easily replace you."

"Yes, sir."

Levi rounded on me. Here it comes!

"Told you. Didn't I?"

Smug asshole.

"We're opening up in twenty. I'm going to grab a red bull before the punters fly in. You want one?" He asked, already making his way to the bar.

"Red Bull with vodka mate," I forced myself to play a more upbeat tune. "Think I'm going to need it."

Levi and I worked in a top restaurant in the heart of Covent Garden. He worked at the bar, and I entertained the guests. 'Zara Blue'. It was one of the prestigious venues you wanted to be seen in! The stage was curved and looked out onto the dining area. As soon as the customer walked into the main doors, there I was! You couldn't miss me. The bar was in my eye line so I could communicate with Levi using a subtle tilt of the head. Or in his case, a display of waving at me like a bloody idiot!

"Can you play Wonderwall?" A drunk in the crowd shouted at me from the restaurant floor. "Come on piano man. Do it for me?"

Christ almighty from Lord above. I'm not kidding when I say that all I saw was a cleavage with maximum support from below. One of these lads, hoping to go home with her after the evening events, was going to be sorely disappointed.

"Sorry guys. I don't do that one." I lied.

Wonderwall was actually one of the many tracks I performed in a covers band I used to be in when we were playing small pub gigs. A band I am no longer connected with, mainly because they didn't have the dedication that I had to music. They wanted to play the 'get a gig quick, despite the venue' and I wanted to make it in the big venues. Sure, being the main pianist in a top end restaurant in the heart of London isn't exactly Wembley, but it's better than a dodgy little pub in the middle of butt fuck nowhere!

"Come on, mate."

A hand was waving in my face. Someone had mounted the stage again.

"Just the chorus, please?"

The look on this guy's face was something out of a scary children's television show.

"Fine." I hate my job right now. "As long as you do the vocals."

"Deal!"

It wasn't an invitation to steal my microphone, but it didn't stop his beer-covered hands from grabbing the SM58. Playing the chorus, I caught Levi at the bar. The smug look on his face said it all. I'd let them walk over me again, succumbing to the pressures of a drunk, nagging audience just for a bit of inner peace and not having to end the evening wrestling for the mic back. What Levi was going to grill me with later, I couldn't care at the present time and moment. The boss was looking on in approval. Seems we have an Oasis fan? Perhaps I should add it back into my collection. If it's keeping Mike off my back then what the hell? Can't hurt.

I ended the song. Yeah, I played the entire song. A thunderous applause resounded throughout the venue and a smile I hadn't felt since before Carrie dumped my arse spread across my face. I checked the time. Another thirty minutes before my break. To hell with it.

"What else do you wanna hear?" I shouted into the microphone, after the drunken beer hand man gave it back.

*****

"Well, well, well," Mike tapped my shoulder. "Where did that come from?" He sat on the bar stool next to me and signalled Levi to get his regular drink. "And I'm not talking about your audience engagement. I'm talking about that smile."

I glanced to my left where both Mike and Levi were resting on the bar, waiting for an answer.

"Mike's got a point, mate. It's been weeks since we saw that look."

"Maybe we've got over Carrie, Levi," Mike said, not even giving me a chance to speak. "Or perhaps this could be the beginning of the end of moping around looking like a lost little puppy."

"I'm not a lost little puppy."

Mike finished his drink and got up. "I beg to differ." He smacked me on the back. "Oh, and before I forget. We have a new member of staff starting with us tomorrow, so," He waved a finger at Levi, "best behaviour. Both of you!"

"As always, Mike." I turned, leaning on the bar as he swayed out of the door toward the kitchen. No doubt to check on what the chef was up to.

"Seriously, mate, that was something else. I can't remember the last time I witnessed you that ecstatic to be on stage. What changed?"

"Honestly?" I shrugged my shoulders. "I gave up trying to control the audience and let them do what they wanted."

"Well, it worked." A blonde woman called for Levi's attention, which he was more than happy about since her boobs were resting on his bar. A clean shot of what was to come. "So get back up there and rock out."

I picked up a bottle of water he had prepped for me. "As much as you can with a classical grand piano."

One shift down and a cab drive later, Levi and I went our separate ways. I, in the room to the left. He, to the right, with the lady from the bar. It'll be about an hour until I get some peace and no doubt I'll be the one who sends her on her way tomorrow morning! Instead of heading to bed, I reminisced about the good old days. Opening a square box labelled band crap. The first object I pull out? An old tattered bandana I used to wear on my right wrist. Don't judge me. I thought it made me look cool. Next, a playlist from one of the best gigs we ever played and right there, halfway down? Wonderwall. I can't deny it. It's a classic nineties track. Instead of sitting at my piano, I picked up my old trusty guitar and strung out a few cords, mumbling the lyrics under my breath. I make a mental note.

Take this playlist to work tomorrow.

*****

"Christ above all that is holy, Ethan." A colleague from the kitchen said. "You look knackered. Slept all last night?"

"If you can call 'trying to sleep' while Levi takes care of business, Ian? No."

"What've you got there?" Ian asks, trying to steal a folder away from me I thought was out of sight. Clearly not.

"Oh, this?" I point at the item in question. "Just thought I'd try out a few other tracks tonight."

Before Ian could say another word, I aimed for the stage to set up. Levi wasn't due until later, which meant I had some chance to practise the songs from my old band in some kind of peace before the doors opened. I'd spent the day searching YouTube for our old band account, playing each video I could find into a suitable version for a pianist. I wasn't planning on changing the entire set. Mike would have my balls in a vice if I did that. It was Christmas, so some seasonal songs had to be played, but I could spice things up in between the cheesy songs we all know and love. Mid practice, my name gets yelled across the venue floor.

"ETHAN!"

"Yes, Mike?"

"You here, now. I need you!"

I closed my folder and did as he commanded. There was no point in arguing with him when he yelled like that. Even though I had come in early to rehearse. Not bend to his every command.

"What's up?"

"I want to introduce you to our new member of staff. Ava."

Ava

I can't tell you how many times I've sat at the bar of 'Zara Blue', wishing I was working on the other side. Sure, you're going to tell me. 'Ava, dreaming about working behind a bar?' Some people get a thrill from it. Mixing cocktails. The rush. Never knowing who you're going to serve next. And at Zara Blue, if you want to make a name for yourself in this business, this is the place to be seen. I knew its reputation throughout London and anyone who's anyone is there. You want a table at this place? You might as well book in for next Christmas because you sure as hell won't get a table this year. I had worked in the cafes, the pubs and the occasional dodgy restaurant, but now I am officially starting my first shift at Zara Blue.

Since I didn't have any uniform yet, I threw on the traditional outfit any new starter would wear. Black fitted chinos with a cute thin belt. A cream top, which was cut down at the front, but not too far that any colleague thought they were in with a shot and some black pumps. I say pumps. They're more like trainer pumps. Pulling my hair back into a high bun and tying a small scarf around it to make it look feminine, I threw my long puffer jacket on and headed out the door, swinging my satchel over my shoulders.

The underground was packed with Londoners heading home, and I was heading out. Office workers were engrossed in their phones and not budging from their seats, which made it amusing when they almost missed their stops. Four stops in and mine was coming into view. Covent Garden. My phone buzzed in my jacket pocket as I rode to the ground floor in the lift. I opened my messages as I marched through the streets to the restaurant.

MIA - Good luck tonight Sis. You are going to be amazing. Have fun and tell me all about it tomorrow, ok. #twinpromise Xx.

AVA - I hope so! I'm a mixture of excitement and

nerves all rolled into one. #twinpromise, I will call as soon as I'm awake in the morning. Love you Xx.

MIA - Not too early, thanks. Love you too Xx.

Mia was five minutes older than me, but treated our sibling bond as if she was five years older. I hadn't seen her for the past two months. She lived in Coventry with her husband, Noah and their kids, Caleb and Elijah. Twin boys aged five. I really should plan a weekend up there when I get some time.

Turning a corner and pocketing my phone, the restaurant came into view. The blue lights that usually shone on the front of the building were off right now. A clear sign they were not open to the public yet. But when they were on? It was like something out of an Ice Queen's castle. Instead of tapping on the door, which I already knew no one was monitoring, I remembered what Mike told me.

"When you arrive, take the alley to the left, make a right turn and you'll find the back entrance"

Left. Right. There it is. STAFF ONLY. I will admit, I let out a little squeal of excitement before I knocked on the door. It didn't take long before someone answered.

"Yeah?" a short, plump man said, looking me up and down.

"Oh, hey." I waved awkwardly, immediately regretting it. "I'm Ava. I'm new. Mike told me_"

"Ava! Yeah!" He threw an arm over my shoulder and guided me into what I could only assume was his kitchen. "The boss told us to expect a newbie this evening." He held his hand out, which was covered in meat sauce. "Name's Ian."

I look down at his hand. Oh my God, I have to touch that. Ugh! Don't think about it Ava, just do it. Fuuuuck, that's gross.

"Ava Barnes. Bar staff."

Ian burst out into laughter. "I like you Ava. Few would have had the balls to shake my hand fresh out of a turkey carcass,"

WTF!

"But you lassie." He wagged his greasy fingers at me,

picking up a towel and passing me another. "You've got balls."

"Thank you?"

"I'm serious. We need a lassie like you on that floor. Give the lads some good old discipline, because let me tell you. They need it sometime."

"Ian? Taste check."

"And that's me. Have fun out there and if you need anything? You come and find me, ok?"

"Sure." I finish cleaning my hands, still being able to feel the inside of the turkey under my nails and try to figure out which door I head towards now. If anywhere, the door from where I can hear music should be about right?

A one-way window 'peep hole' was at the perfect height on the double door, which led into the main area of the venue. I should have known. Every time I'd visit, I would stare at the gold plated section of the doors and wonder how many times the kitchen staff had their noses pressed up against it when a critic or a high diner was about to taste their masterpiece.

You can do this Ava. Deep breath in and out. You've got this.

Swinging the door open, I came face to face with my future. Zara Blue's restaurant and venue floor. One issue though. Despite the regular pianist practicing, where was everyone else? I had turned up on the correct day, right? I was about to walk back into the kitchen and ask Ian if I'd made a mistake when a voice spoke behind me.

"Ava," Mike, the owner, boss, and top dog, said. "Sorry I'm late meeting you. Bloody cat brought home a mouse and let me tell you, the wife was not amused by the mess. Please, let me fix you a coffee before we get into it. I have a feeling from looking at tonight's guest list. We're all going to need all the caffeine we can handle."

"Oh, thank you."

Mike guided me to the bar, where I would spend most of my time.

"How d'you have it? Latte? Americano? Espresso? Sugar? Syrup?"

"Hazelnut latte, if it's not too much trouble?"

"One thing we pride ourselves on here, Ava."

Mike began working the coffee like a pro. Never in my career had the boss offered to make me a drink.

"We look out for one another. We're not just working at the same restaurant, we're family and over time I think you'll see that more than anything" He planted what looked like the most elegant and beautiful latte in front of me. "And that includes making and knowing each other's coffee preferences."

I lent down and took a whiff. "Oh, my days, that smells divine."

"Should taste it too." He turned to face the back of the bar, making a coffee for himself. "ETHAN!"

From his volume, I almost spilt the entire contents of my mug all over my cream top.

"You here, now. I need you!"

Checking I hadn't made a complete mess of myself, I looked up to find the pianist walking toward me. He wore an open dark green, white and black chequered shirt with a white t-shirt beneath. Black jeans and a pair of white and black skater trainers. A bandana wrapped around his right wrist and a cap taming his dark brown hair. I'd heard him play before when I was out for drinks with my girlfriends, and we admired his talents and his obvious good looks. But up close? This man was going to make it hard to concentrate on my workload.

"Yeah? What's up?" Ethan said. The strain in his voice sounded annoyed. Mike had obviously broken his attention.

"I want to introduce you to our new member of staff. Ava."

He looked at me, and I swear I made a noise that could only be described as a 'oooh' when I looked into his brown eyes. I'm in trouble!

"Ava will work the bar with Levi." Mike pointed at Ethan. "Watch that arsehole for me, will you? You know what he's like."

"You don't have to tell me twice. I have to live with him." Ethan said. His voice just added another 'oooh,' to escape.

"I know you're busy, but I have to sort out the waiting staff rota. We have some big names tonight."

Mike passed Ethan a coffee. Black coffee. Check! "Can I ask you to show Ava the ropes? Please?"

I swear Ethan did a double take at Mike saying 'please'.

"Sure."

Mike went on his way, leaving me with Ethan. He sat on the stool next to me, fidgeting with his coffee mug. There was something underlying about this man, and I couldn't quite put my finger on it.

"So, welcome to Zara."

"Yeah. I mean, thanks." Smooth! Delightful conversation so far. Think Ava, think. "I've, er, I've heard you play before."

"Really?"

"You're, like, so good."

Jesus! Really? I sound like a fan.

"That actually means a lot to hear you say that."

I take a sip of coffee. "You must hear it every night?"

"You'd be surprised. Usually the punters are just shouting requests, thinking I'm a human jukebox." I let out an unattractive snort laugh which he noticed. I'm rewarded with the most stunning smile I have ever seen in my life. "I'm serious, which is why I'm going to try something new tonight."

"Like what?"

"And ruin the surprise? You'll have to wait and see. Now," He stood up and offered me his arm. "I should do as the boss asked, and warn you about Levi?"

"Levi? Is that the guy who's usually behind the bar?"

"Yeah, my best mate and an absolute sex pest!"

*****

Ethan showed me around the entire building, from the top floor to the basement. How he thought I was going to remember everything was a miracle. Every member of staff we passed he introduced to me and they welcomed me with a full smile and friendly hug. I was understanding what Mike said about this place feeling like family.

Coming full circle, we found ourselves back in the main area where staff were dressing the tables with glasses, Christmas themed decorations and bottles of champagne on ice. Not the cheap stuff you'd find in the local superstore. Oh, no. We're talking about a thousand pound bottle of champagne. Mike said we'd need all the caffeine in the world with tonight's guest list. He wasn't fibbing. Anyone who can afford to dress each table with expensive champagne could be a handful.

"This is where I have to leave you." Ethan said.

Did I just sense a hint of sadness in his voice?

I clung to him a little tighter. He must have thought I was nervous, not that I couldn't be without the scent of his cologne for a second, because he faced me and placed his hands on either side of my arms.

"You're going to be amazing and if you need anything." He pointed to the stage. "I'll be right there."

"Ava?" Mike's voice broke my focus while I was remembering the shade of Ethan's eyes. "You ready?"

Ethan

Focus, focus, focus!

This was not how this evening was meant to go. I'd planned to rock the pants of tonight's guests with the playlist from my band days. Not spend the time staring at Ava behind the bar, where I can clearly see Levi trying to flirt with her.

When Mike called me over, I assumed it was going to be something like, 'Don't be a dull prick tonight Ethan. One word about Carrie and you are toast!' Not 'This is Ava'. The most beautiful woman I think I have ever laid eyes on. Ava's delicate features and rosy cheeks were to die for and when she looked at me, I forgot all about Carrie. Her light brown hair was tied up in such an adorable bun and her blue eyes? My God. Listen to me? I sound like a thirteen love stricken school boy.

I was at a loss for what to say at first. Part of me wanted to swing at Mike for putting me in that position after a break-up, but the other half wanted to thank him. Thank the Lord she wasn't as awkward as I was, or was she? She said 'You're, like, so good.', clearly a 'I can't think of what else to say here' line. Forget it Ethan. She's gorgeous and you're a mess. A big slump of emotional mess that shouldn't even be thinking about a colleague in that way, anyway!

The restaurant floor was busier than I've ever seen it. Each table was taken. The atmosphere was alive with excitement and energy. Laughter and smiles from everyone in the room lifted my own spirits. Tonight's evening show was going to be good. I can just tell. Right now though, as they destroyed the meals, I was stuck to playing the festive tunes. Levi and Ava can fill them with the booze. Ian and his team will fill them with delicious food while I fill them with the festive spirit.

Looking up, I saw Levi waving a hand at me. Ah, my 'Five more minutes until your break' wave. I spoke gently into the microphone, which had been thoroughly cleaned after the drunk man from last night.

"This will be my last song before I take a quick break." A few faces looked my way, "I rarely do this, but, any requests?"

A hand shot up from the middle of the room and a curvaceous woman with long, dark brown hair stood up.

"It's beginning to look a lot like Christmas!"

She has taste.

"Sure. What's your name?"

"Emma."

"Ok Emma, this one's for you." I played the opening riff and I couldn't help but smile at what I saw out of the corner of my eye. Her friends got up and swayed along with her. Arms wrapped around each other. A blonde, another brunette, and Emma. Their partners stayed seated, watching them dance as their desserts were being presented by the kitchen staff. Each one of them geared up for the night of their lives.

They sang along to every word, not once trying to steal my microphone, and on the last note they gave me a round of applause like I was playing the Albert Hall. If only every night had punters like them.

Jumping from the stage, I made my way toward what I knew was waiting for me. My usual. A nice cold bottle of water and a slice of cake!

"Hell of a set tonight Ethan, what changed from your usual bummed out self?"

I enjoyed a long sip before I answered Levi. "Had a rummage around while you were 'busy' last night," I couldn't help notice the amusing look on Ava's face. Either she got my air quote reference, or Levi had been bragging.

"Found some of the old band setlists and thought I'd see how it still came across."

"Well, whatever you're doing, it's not only working the crowds tonight, it's a sure distraction from Carrie."

"And you saying her name really helps."

"Who's Carrie?" Ava asked, drying a beer glass fresh out of the washer.

The panicked expression on my face said it all, and she saw it.

"Forget I asked_"

"Carrie," Levi. No boundaries and certainly not holding back, "was the woman who dumped his ass last week."

I rolled my eyes. "Thank you, Levi."

"What?"

Ava looked at me with pity and sadness and a hint of relief? "Why?"

Ok, I'm not thick, I can play Mozart from memory, but was that a smile I saw her trying to hide? Is she glad I was dumped? Or am I looking too much into this? Roll with it Ethan.

"Usual things when you break up. She wanted to explore different options. Said she felt I was holding her back, that my position here would never be enough, so on and so on." I waved my hand dismissively.

"Sounds like you dodged a bullet." Ava said, picking up another glass. "If I was dumped by someone who sounds that high maintenance, I'd thank my stars I didn't have to put up with whatever bullshit they were going to put me down with now _" Ava trailed off when she saw us staring at her. "Sorry, I overstepped. I have a habit of speaking my mind. What I should've said was, 'oh mate, sorry'. That's more like it, right?"

Levi was the first to throw his head back and laugh. "We have been trying to tell him exactly that for the past six months!"

"Have you fuck?" I protested.

"You know we have Ethan. Every time you came in looking beaten, Mike and I would tell you. It's Carrie. She always put your job down, expected you to be her constant knight in shining armour and whenever you were having an 'Ethan Day', she'd throw a fit."

"I'm sorry, I'm sorry." Ava shook her head. "What's an Ethan Day?"

Why are we telling a woman I've just met all my secrets and habits? Ugh!

"I have days when I don't feel great." I tap my head. "Mentally."

She smiled softly at me and lay her hand on my arm. Her touch was so gentle, it was like someone running a feather over my arm.

"Believe me, I know exactly where you're coming from. Some days all I want to do is hide under my duvet and watch reruns." Her concern over my well-being lit my soul on fire. "Maybe we could hide together one day?"

"Like, the pair of you? Under the duvet?" Levi pointed at us. "Together?"

"What?" The shade of pink that rose on Ava's face was adorable. "No, no, that's not what I meant. I mean." She covered her face with her hands as Mike spared her the embarrassment.

"Ethan!" Mike shouted from the back office. "Two minutes!"

I picked up my water bottle. "Maybe this is a conversation for another time." I couldn't help myself. I gave her a sideways grin and a wink and made my way back to the stage. As I let my fingers find the keys, I glanced her way. Levi had his back to me, whispering something as Ava looked up and caught my eye. What was going on?

The rest of the evening continued late into the night and without sounding like I'm trying to blow my trumpet, I rocked! The crowd loved me. Not once did anyone try to steal the mic, they only mounted the stage to take a selfie with me mid song. Nearing the end of my last song, I saw Ava watching me. She was singing along to every word and the smile she wore when I delivered the final note lit up the room.

She is beautiful.

Climbing from the stage, Emma and her friends bounced over to me. They had most definitely had one too many, but they could still hold a sentence.

Emma engulfed me in a hug. "That was amazing!"

"Oh, thank you." A hug and a compliment after my set. This was new.

"I don't suppose you take bookings, do you?"

"Well, I haven't for a few years, not since I've worked here."

"But you'd consider it?"

"To be honest with you, Emma, I'm not sure why you'd want to book me?"

"Are you kidding?" Emma smacked the side of my arm. This changed quickly. "You are incredible and just the artist I'm looking for."

"I'm sorry, I'm not following."

"Emma is getting married next year," her blonde

friend said. "And she's trying to ask if she can book you for entertainment during the sit down dinner? Aren't you Emma?"

"Yes!" Emma nodded. "Yes, I am. Thank you Lucy."

So one friend is called Lucy. Noted.

I looked down at my feet, feeling not only honoured to be considered to play Emma's wedding, but nervous all at once. I hadn't played a real 'gig' since I left the band.

"I appreciate the offer, but_"

Emma lay her hand on my arm. "You don't have to say yes now, just consider it." She gave me one of her business cards. "April 19th, next year. It would mean the world to me, and Tom. Think about it. Please?"

Glancing down at her card, I smiled. I met her pleading face. "Sure."

She clapped in excitement.

"Yay! Thank you." Her friend Lucy began dragging her away. "Speak to you soon!"

"Speak soon Emma." Playing with the card in between my fingers, I waved goodbye to the rest of their party before placing it in the back of my phone case.

Levi approached the stage and lent his elbows on the raised floor. He was wearing a grin that looked smug as fuck.

"So, you wanna tell me what that was all about? She seems very interested. Just as much as Ava seems to be."

"Emma asked me to play at her wedding." Wait! What did he just say? "Hold up. Ava seems to be what?"

"Oh, please, mate." He hopped onto the stage. "It's so obvious Ethan. She kept watching you the entire night. Playing with her hair when you were speaking? Turned the shade of a beetroot when she suggested you share a duvet?" He jumped up onto the stage and lay his hands on my shoulders as I packed my setlist away. "She likes you and I think you might have a little thing for her too."

Great. I am going to be hearing about this until I do something about it. Which, may I add, I am not ready to do.

"Yeah, she's adorable, but Carrie and I just broke up,

and I still love her. How can I think about making a move on Ava if I'm still het up on Carrie?"

Levi smacked his hands together, making an almighty crack in my left ear. "So you admit it! You like her back?"

"How can someone not like her, Levi? Look at her," I carefully adjusted my seating so Ava was in my sight line. "She's stunning. She's fun. She has the most adorable smile." I let out a long sigh. "But it would be unfair."

"How?"

"Because of Carr_"

"Say that woman's name one more time and I swear I will make a move on Ava and steal your chance to be happy!"

"Have I told you how much of a dick you can be?"

"Never enough Ethan, never enough."

Ava

Tonight was incredible! Everything and more. The atmosphere in the restaurant from my new work colleagues was like nothing I had experienced before. They invited me in with open arms and I already feel part of the family. Levi kindly took me under his wing and supported me for the first hour when the doors opened, but he soon realised I didn't need babysitting. I'd worked bars at festivals, hotels, rundown dives in the middle of butt fuck nowhere. I had my bartender skills down to a tea. The only thing I needed him for was when I couldn't figure out the till, or where a certain glass was. Apart from that, it was plain sailing. And then there was the view. If I hadn't made it obvious before, by suggesting Ethan and I share a duvet, I certainly laid the final coat of cement for everyone to see. I couldn't keep my eyes off him, and Levi knew it. During one song, he whispered to me.

"Listen, Ava." He turned to his back on the stage. "I can see you're into Ethan, but I have to tell you something."

"What is it?"

"Go slow. He's still hurting from the recent breakup."

"Carrie?"

"Yeah." Levi let out a sigh. "He? He planned on proposing this Christmas. She? She had other plans."

I cover my mouth with my hands as I let out a gasp. "Poor guy."

The look of concern was written all over Levi's face, and I realised these two are more than friends. They're more like brothers. Brothers who look out for one another, no matter what.

I tapped Levi's arm. "I understand and anyway, we've only met. Would be weird to make a move on someone I've just met."

*****

"Ladies and gents," Mike said, holding up a beer and tapping it with a spoon to get our attention. "Can I have your attention, please?" He pointed to where I sat with

Ethan and Levi. "That means you too Levi."

"Sorry boss." He dropped his phone and paid attention.

"Tonight has been a massive success, and I want to thank every one of you. The guests this evening were singing your praises as they left. We certainly made a good impression on them, and they are the sort of people we want to be attracting. A comment from them about us? That will bring in the cash, if you know what I mean?"

"What was so special about them Mike?" A voice from the back called out. I don't think I've officially met this voice yet.

"Where have you been living Alex? Under a rock?" Mike said, rubbing a hand over his face. "Tonight we hosted a multi-million company. The bosses of one of the biggest software companies in the city, and I'm pretty sure I saw Ethan over there chatting with them as they left."

"I was?" Ethan said, looking as dumbfounded as Alex was.

"Whatever you all did, I am thrilled with the service you provided."

Was it me, or were we all being a little thick not to realise who we were serving? Me? I was focused on the entertainment and I'm not going to hide that fact. The way Ethan controlled the stage made me smile every time I stole a glance, but I had to remind myself of what Levi said. He was still heartbroken. The last thing I want to do is make a move on someone who's not ready to be in a relationship yet. That doesn't mean I can't appreciate him from a distance? Right?

"Ava?"

Ethan gently tapped my arm. Oh, God his hands feel good. Damn him and his gentle caress. I'm screwed.

"Yeah?"

"We were just talking about what to do on Monday?"

"Monday?"

"The restaurant is closed Mondays. Me and Levi were just talking about grabbing a few drinks." He said, pulling on his jacket. "See where the day goes. You in?"

I don't know why I took a living age to respond.

Probably because I've just met these guys, and I had just told myself not to get too involved with Ethan until he was ready, but looking into his eyes, I found it hard to obey my rule.

"Sounds like a date." I clicked my forefinger and thumb together, finishing the awkward as hell move with a finger gun at him.

What a loser!

"Ok then." Ethan laughed at my corny move. "What's your number?"

"Pardon?"

He waved his phone at me. "So we know where to meet tomorrow?"

Floor, if you could open up right now, that would be great!

"Of course." I took his phone, adding my number. I clicked 'add contact' and wrote my name. Ava Sanders. I hovered over the 'x'. Should I? Is that too much? Will it scare him off? Fuck it!

'Ava Saunders x'

He looked at the screen, and the smile he gave me made my heart melt. God damn!

"Tomorrow then."

"Tomorrow."

*****

When I agreed to take this job, I knew it was going to be demanding. I had a reputation to live up to. Zara Blue had always and will always be the place to be seen, and I certainly saw it in a whole new light tonight. And it was amazing! The atmosphere, the buzz, the banter, the food, the staff. The pianist. Walking to the tube station, I replayed everything I remembered saying to Ethan, praying I hadn't made a complete idiot of myself and apart from the weird finger gun, I think I passed? My mouth is usually the first to fail me. Oh, no! The duvet! Yep, how could I have forgotten that? Levi almost died laughing at my embarrassment. Thank the Lord Mike arrived before I said anything else.

Ethan and Levi left ahead of me, as I wanted to catch up with Mike. Just the usually new starter procedure.

How'd I do? Any tips? Blah, blah. Mike had nothing to say but praise.

"You're one I'm going to monitor Ava. You certainly know what you're doing and if Levi doesn't watch it, you'll end up bar manager before you know it."

In the comfort of my one bedroom studio flat, tucked under the plush duvet with extra blankets, I reached for my favourite book and opened the pages to where my bookmark was. Page one hundred and seventy-six. I was about to enjoy my book boyfriend for a few chapters when my phone sounded. I abandoned the book and opened my messages.

"Mia, whatever it is, it can wait until... Ethan?"

ETHAN - Hey Ava, it's Ethan. Realised you hadn't taken our numbers, wouldn't want you to think some random person was calling you tomorrow!

AVA - That's very considerate of you

ETHAN - You're welcome. Hope you had a good first shift tonight?

AVA - I did thanks. Everyone was so welcoming and the entertainment wasn't too shabby either ;)

What am I doing? Stop text flirting! What did you tell yourself earlier?

ETHAN - As long as you enjoyed it, then I did my job. X

Is that a kiss? Did he post a kiss?

ETHAN - As for tomo, is midday ok? Waterloo Station? Thought we'd hit up the Christmas markets on Southbank?

AVA - Actually sounds perfect. I need to get my sister a gift. See you tomorrow? X

ETHAN - Night Ava x

*****

BUZZ! BUZZ! BUZZ!

"No." I reached to my side to silence the alarm clock that was nagging my ass out of bed. "Five more minutes."

BUZZ! BUZZ! BUZZ!

"OK, ok, ok!" Swinging the sheets back, I reached up, stretching my limbs and enjoyed a satisfying yawn. The temptation to throw myself back in bed was overwhelming, but then I remembered. Drinks with Ethan and Levi. Bouncing off the bed, I caught my reflection. Dear Lord, bed hair and last night's mascara. Nice! Ignoring my phone vibrating, no doubt a message from Mia wanting to know how last night went, I chose my most comfortable outfit before taking a shower. I always liked to get what I was going to wear prepared beforehand. It was a habit both Mia, and I picked up from our Mum. Loving the feel of the hot water on my skin, I reached for the shampoo as I let my mind wander. What on earth was I going to get Mia for a Christmas present? Her husband, Noah, was easy to buy for. Book vouchers and a nice whiskey. But Mia? Mia was a nightmare. One minute she's into a certain style, then she'd hate it, then she throws you off by changing her entire wardrobe when you think you have her sussed! When it comes to buying Mia a gift, she's more like a stranger than a twin.

Towel drying my hair, and blasting it with the hairdryer, I put on basic makeup and got dressed. Classic stone washed skinny jeans. Thigh high flat boots. Oversized mauve jumper and matching scarf. Topped off with my loyal puffer jacket. If it's cold out there, I wouldn't know about it. I checked the time. Ten Forty Five. Half an hour tube journey. Enough time to grab a coffee and give myself a talking too about not flirting with Ethan before we meet up? Perfect.

Finding the nearest cafe, I put in my order and took

my glorious beverage to find a seat within the station. I knew the lads would come on a different tube line to what I arrived on, so it made sense to wait near the entrance to their underground. The Bakerloo line. The dodgy brown one. If you've ever seen a map of the London Underground, you'd agree with me. After finishing my coffee, I checked the time again. Twelve fifteen.

"Where are they?" I was about to text Ethan when I heard my name being yelled across the station. Levi was waving like an idiot with a blonde on his arm. Someone got lucky last night?

Ethan got to me first and, with no warning, wrapped me in a warm embrace. Holy shit, he smelt amazing. Whatever cologne he was wearing, it was working.

"Sorry we're a little late." He said, tilting his head back to the reason they were running late. "Someone was preoccupied."

"It's ok. I've not been here long."

He caught my take away cup.

"Long enough to finish a coffee?" He took the cup from me and threw it in the nearest bin. "First drinks are on me, ok?"

I playfully nudged him. "No complaining from me."

Flirting rule, broken, already. Entirely. Smashed. A speck of dust in the distance!

"Who's your friend Levi?"

I couldn't believe my eyes when I saw Levi blush. I'd known this guy for less than a day and I already figured out he's not usually the kind to blush because of a 'friend'.

"Ava, meet Melanie." Levi said, with more than a little strain in his voice. "Melanie, this is Ava. Ava started working at Zara last night and has settled in nicely already."

The look Melanie gave me was priceless. Touch my man and I'll end you. Either way, I extended my hand toward her manicured pink nails. I would not be the bitch here.

"Nice to meet you, Melanie."

She looked at my hand, and I instantly wanted to punch her.

"Hi." she said before pulling her hand back.

AWKWARD!

"Shall we head to the market?" Ethan said, breaking the silence that we all felt.

He let Levi and Melanie lead the way. He placed a hand on the top of my back and leaned in closer to me, his voice dropping to a whisper.

"He met her a couple of nights ago at work. Let's just say it's a one-night stand that went wrong." I sniggered in amusement. "Hasn't been able to get rid of her. I hate her as much as you do."

"I don't hate her."

"Come on, it's written all over your face."

There was no point in denying it. He was right. I wasn't keen on her and Ethan wasn't making any attempt to hide his dislike, either. We hung back on the walk to the market, trying our best not to laugh every time Levi looked around with a pleading look of help on his face.

"I don't understand." I said as we rounded the corner to end up in the heart of a very busy Christmas market. "If it was a one-night stand, why's she still hanging around?"

Ethan walked backwards, facing me. "Pretty sure she doesn't think that, and when she turned up at Zara the next evening, we knew he had a problem."

"Wait!" I steered Ethan before he crashed into a child. "She was waiting for him? At Zara? That screams stalker vibes."

He burst into a fit of laughter. "I know! But being the unhelpful friend I am, I let it run its course, and here we are. Levi is now in an unwanted relationship. Serves him right."

"How?"

"I already told you yesterday he's a sex pest. A massive flirt. It was only going to be a matter of time before it backfired." He gestured to the happy couple. "And there you have it. I will never let him live this down."

I stopped and placed a hand on my hip. "Wow, you are such an amazing friend."

"The best kind!"

He looped my arm through his, like he did the day before when he gave me a tour of the restaurant. When I looked down, he explained the gesture.

"It's busy. Wouldn't want to lose you in the crowd."

Ethan

She hasn't dropped my arm yet. That must mean it's going well, right?

My nerves were shot when I woke up this morning. Yeah, Levi's idea that we spend the day off together in order for us to get to know one another better worked like a charm. But now that I'm here with Ava, I'm a nervous wreck. I just hope the techniques I use when I'm on stage are hiding the fact that I'm terrified. The way she's holding my arm, I feel like I'm home and that is not ok. I can't hurt this perfect woman. Levi gave me a pep talk this morning over our usual breakfast; coffee and bagels with peanut butter and sliced banana. #SoMascline!

"I know you're nervous Ethan, but remember these words. She. Likes. You. And You. Like. Her." He took another bite of his bagel, speaking with a mouthful. There was one way to get rid of Melanie, because that was disgusting. "Just see where the day takes you and do NOT mention Carrie. Understand me?"

The guy was right, of course, and I had to rein in the ex's name. Oh, yeah, he also added, right after saying her name, that we are not to mention her by name ever again.

"Ethan, look."

"Huh?'

I was so far into my own thoughts I forgot where we were until Ava took a right, dragging me toward a photo booth. It was set up to look like a Christmas scene. Low budget, but still a seasonal scene.

"We should do it. Correction, we are doing it."

With no chance to respond, she dropped her arm from around mine. I'll admit my heart dropped when she let go, but sparks soon returned when she laced her fingers through mine instead. Shit, I'm screwed.

"Photo for the happy couple?" The photographer asked.

"Oh, we're not..." Ava tried to wave her hands, instead lifting our interwoven hands up together.

"Could have fooled me. A good-looking pair like you?"

Thank you, Mr Snaps. Way to make this even more awkward than it already is.

"Now, you." He clicked his fingers at me. "Sit."

"What now?

He directed me to a chair dressed in red sheets among a fluffy white carpet? Blanket? I don't know what it is, but the amount of dirty marks from people's shoes made it in dire need of a wash. I sat, awaiting the next instruction.

"What's your name, love?" Mr Snaps asked.

"Ava."

"Go sit on your man's knee Ava and 'pretend' you're in love."

He dropped his voice to a whisper as Ava approached me. He may have thought he couldn't have been heard, but my ears had been trained to hear my band mates talking to me mid set, during the song. Nothing got past me, especially when he said 'which you blindly are'.

"This ok?" Ava asked me.

"Uh yeah, sure." I tapped my knee.

Christ almighty Ethan. Good move!

I swear she looked as nervous as I did. Flicking her hair over her right shoulder, which smelt delicious, she sat on my right knee and draped her arm around my shoulders. Should I do the same? Should I lay a hand on her leg?

Mr Snaps waited. He raised an eyebrow at me. Then I realised what he was doing. He knew I liked this woman. He was giving me an inning. An opportunity to get up and close to her, to hold her in my arms. To feel her warm embrace. What a legend. I may not be ready to commit yet, but why shouldn't I make the most of it. It was her idea to do this. I'm doing it.

"Lean forward?" I asked her.

She did. I wrapped my arm around her waist and confidently lay my hand on her leg. Her sharp intake of her breath told me everything I needed to know. Levi was right. She did like me. I pulled her close and glanced at the photographer. He subtly gave me a thumbs up.

"Right into the lens to start guys." He took a couple of shots of us, smiling at him. "Now, get to know each other and ignore me."

I turned and found Ava's blue eyes staring into mine. She was so close. Close enough to kiss her, to enjoy the feel of her lips pressed against mine. Was she thinking the same thing? Her eyes dropped to my mouth. She was! I leaned in, naturally, wanting a taste.

"That's a wrap guys."

BASTARD!

"Write your email down here and I'll get these edited and sent over by the end of the day."

Ava stood up, breaking the connection to write her details down. Mr Snaps approached me.

"You've got something that could be really special there, mate, don't lose it." He smacked the back of my shoulder.

"And who are you to tell me what I should do?"

"Someone who's been in your position before and messed it up." He tapped his camera. "These have turned out brilliantly."

"Ethan?"

We both looked up at where Ava had called from.

This time I smacked Mr Snap's shoulder. "Thanks mate."

She didn't take my hand this time, instead choosing to type at lightning speed on her phone. Whoever she was texting, it must have been someone special.

"Where'd you two get to?" Levi asked with a stern 'the fuck have you been, you left me with the cling-on,' tone in his voice.

His face was an absolute picture of annoyance.

"Sorry mate, we stopped by a photo booth."

Levi looked between the pair of us. "Oh yeah? Anything else?"

Christ, this guy will not leave it alone until I tell him. Later.

"No."

"Bullshit."

I scooted close to him. I didn't want Ava hearing me sound like a teenager, and I certainly didn't want Melanie knowing anything about my private life. Anything about my life, in fact.

"Tell you later, alone."

"I want a drink." Melanie announced. "Sugar plum,

can we get a drink?"

Sugar plum? Pet names already? Levi needs to dump this girl sooner than later. He ignored the smirk that I was not trying to hide on my face, instead flipping me off from behind his unwanted girlfriend. Was that aimed at me? Or her? Probably both.

"Ava?" I taped her elbow, breaking her concentration with the screen. "Drink?"

"Huh? Oh, yeah, sure. I can do that."

"If you need a few more minutes to finish up-"

"No, no." She pressed send and placed her phone in her back pocket. "I'm good. I was just texting my sister. Where are we going?"

We followed Melanie to a nearby bistro on the Thames. She was a royal pain, but she knew where the best places to enjoy a coffee with a view was. We sat around a table overlooking the river. Right behind Ava's head stood the London Eye, slowly turning to give the riders a view of the city. I let out a long sigh. Carrie and I had enjoyed a champagne ride only a few months ago. I rented a booth to ourselves so we could enjoy the peace while sipping on champagne. The evening sunset made the city glow. It was a sight to see, and I found it hard to look away from the eye. A hand appeared in front of me, snapping its fingers to bring me back to reality. Levi was giving me the death stare. He always knew what I was thinking about, and at that moment, I was thinking about Carrie.

"Oi, dipshit?"

Insulting me, very grown up Levi.

"Usual?"

"Sure, yeah, but I owe you a drink so these are on me." I opened my phone to take down a drinks order in my notes. "What's everyone else having?"

Drinks order in hand, I lent on the bar and awaited my turn to be served. I wasn't about to signal the bar staff. I see that happen all the time at Zara Blue and it winds our staff up like nothing else. Instead, I opened my messages and began a chat with my elder sister. Chrissy.

ETHAN - Sis, need to chat, you free?

CHRISSY - What's up?

Chrissy and I have and always will be there for each other. No matter the time of day or whatever we're doing. Last time it was Chrissy that needed me when the company she worked for went into liquidation, resulting in her being unemployed until she landed a new job. Trying to find an opening in her field as a biochemist was hard, but she was soon picked up by a medical company in the East End of London.

ETHAN - There's this new woman at work, Ava, and I think I like her.

CHRISSY - So? You're single now, what's stopping you? Does she like you?

ETHAN - I think so. We had a moment earlier.

CHRISSY - A moment?

ETHAN - I was sure she wanted me to kiss her.

CHRISSY - OMG!! Did you?

ETHAN - No, we were distracted and I don't think I'm ready yet.

CHRISSY - Carrie? Right?

ETHAN - : (

CHRISSY - Bro, she's long gone and frankly, I'm glad of it. She was using you for your kindness. Carrie was bad news and you know it, but I know what you're like. You don't want to hurt this woman, am I right?

ETHAN - You're always right. What would you do?

CHRISSY - For starters, trust nothing Levi tells

you. Play it cool, little bro, and if it's meant to happen, then it will. Ride the waves, you get me?

ETHAN - I get you. Hey, you and Mariah coming home for Christmas this year?

Mariah, Chrissy's fiancee and Chrissy, had spent the last couple of years at her parents as her dad had been going through chemo. At long last he was cancer free and her parents took a Christmas holiday to see the northern lights and enjoy the season, just the two of them. A trip that was at the top of their list when Mariah's dad was well enough.

CHRISSY - You have the honour! See you next week at Mum and Dads. Oh, and I want to see a picture of this Ava who has you all tied up in knots.

Ava

Levi needs to grow a pair and dump this woman already, and I know I will be the one to do it. It's clear that my presence in this trio will be the one that speaks to the wannabe ex girlfriends on Levi's behalf, because Ethan is doing a fine job at ignoring everything Melanie is saying. Is it weird that I find his ignorance to this woman adorably cute? It's been two days, but I can already call them my friends but I am finding it hard to keep my eyes and hands to myself around Ethan. The way he confidently laid his hand on my leg when we posed for the photos made me shiver. I hope he didn't notice, but when he looked at me, I was a puddle of an emotional mess at his feet, or his lap in that case. I'd looked into his eyes before, but not that close up and I swear when I lost control, him after and glanced at his lips, wanting a taste. I'm sure I saw a twitch at the corner of his mouth like he was thinking the same thing. Shit, I have no self-control around this man. I can't throw myself at him after he just had his heart broken by the woman he hoped to marry? Can I? I don't want to be the rebound.

"What do you think Ava?"

I was so far away in my own thoughts, again; I didn't catch a word Ethan said to me.

"What?"

Ethan smiled at me and lent his arms on the table. "We were talking about what songs I should try out this week? Levi thinks I should mix it up"

"What's wrong with what you're doing already? I like what you've got."

Levi picked up his drink and mumbled into the glass.

"Bet you do." He thought I didn't hear him, but I caught it. Clear as day, which meant Ethan did, too.

"I suppose it wouldn't hurt throwing in some classics." Ethan turned on me again. "What's your favourite style of music? Favourite song? I could learn it. Surprise you one night."

You already have surprised me.

"Oh, umm." I shrugged, unable to think up a favourite song when put on the spot. "Why is this so hard!"

Melanie moaned, "Ugh, just pick one."

"I will, when it comes to mind. Right now, I can't think of anything. Is that ok?" I said through gritted teeth.

Her face was a picture of disgust. She obviously wasn't used to someone speaking to her is such a 'please fuck the back off' mode. She rounded on Levi and jabbed a finger in my direction.

"Levi! Are you going to allow that?"

"Allow what?" He said from behind his glass, trying to hide his amusement.

"Allow that kind of behaviour toward your girlfriend!"

"Who ever said you were his girlfriend?" Ethan leant back in his chair, reaching behind and resting his hand on the back of his head. "As far as I heard, you were just sleeping together, for the night."

Ethan - ONE

Melanie - ZERO

I think I've just fallen for this man even more. That was the best #MicDrop moment I have ever witnessed!

"LEVI!" Melanie stood up in a huff. "Do something! NOW!"

"Ok, sure." Levi stood up to match her stance.

I sat back and leant close to Ethan, dropping my voice to a whisper. "Did we just line this break up for him?"

"Yeah, and now he owes us for life. Next rounds on him." He offered his fist, which I dumped in celebration. "Relax, and enjoy the show."

"You're a pain in my ass, Melanie." Levi went straight in with it. I'm actually a little proud right now. "You're high maintenance and I never wanted a relationship, so where you got that idea from is beyond me."

She put a hand on her hip. "EXCUSE ME?"

"I told you before we left Zara I wasn't interested and yet you turned up at our work the next day thinking we're all lovey dovey."

I'll admit, both Ethan and I cringed at that part.

"So do me a favour and find someone else you'll have you for the holidays because sweetheart, it's not me."

Melanie's jaw dropped and hit the floor. She looked at

me and Ethan, pretending to look in opposite directions with our mouths firmly shut. From both the urge to comment and to stop the laughter from escaping. She picked up her bag, swinging it over her shoulder in a huff.

"Alright, ok, fine!" She stomped her foot.

She's actually having a 'throw all the toys out of the pram huff,' right now. Why aren't we filming this? This is viral material!

"You work for a shitty restaurant anyway, and your cocktails are crap and YOU." She turned on Ethan. "You never played the song I requested, either. You both suck. You all suck. I'm better off with none of you, you sucky little suckers." As if on queue we all began applauding her Oscar winning strop. She looked disgusted, flipped her hair and stormed off.

"Hey Melanie." Levi called after her.

"What!"

"Merry Christmas." He winked at her, just to rub more salt in the wound, and sat down with the biggest sigh I had ever heard.

From behind, we could hear Melanie mumbling something as she fucked off into the distance.

"I don't know how to thank you guys."

"Another round wouldn't go amiss?" Ethan slid the empty glasses toward him. "Then we'll talk about what comes next."

Accepting the hint, Levi grinned and did as Ethan asked. Alone once more, sitting on the edge of the Thames, I felt a smile spread across my face.
Ethan nudged me. "What's got you?"

I sighed. "Just thinking. I've known you two no longer than a day and you've made me feel so welcome. At work and," I gesture around the table, "out of work too. I suppose I just feel really blessed."

"Well," Ethan laid his hand on mine. "I'm glad you feel that way."

He held my gaze and that same feeling I felt when we were at the photo booth returned. Does he feel it too? His eyes search mine as if they are trying to look into my soul. I feel the pull again. Levi said not to rush it, but I can't deny the feelings I have for this man.

"Ethan, I,"

"Drinks are up!"

Damn you Levi!

People's timings are really on point today! Ethan moved quicker than I liked, opening the gap between us, and coughed to regain his posture. From those few seconds and the ones we shared at the booth, I knew. He was into me as well.

*****

Two weeks after my first day at Zara Blue and life couldn't be better. I had the job I had always wanted, and colleagues who were like family. People were actually asking my advice on drinks and where things were. Since that trip to the market, Ethan and I continued to flirt, but I constantly remind myself that he's still healing and if I want to be with this gorgeous man, I need to give him the space he needs to recover. Every time I catch his gaze, it makes my imagination run wild.

"Ava! Levi shouted, stopping my visualisation of Ethan from going into overdrive and imagining him kissing and making love to me. "Heads up!"

Catching the beer glass that was coming in my direction, I dried the remaining water droplets and placed it upside down under the bar.

Christmas day was only a couple of days away, and every night was a full house. Not a single table was free, so if anyone 'popped' in on the off chance, there wasn't a chance in hell. A table at Zara Christmas week? Should have booked it last year!

"Round up people!" Mike shouted from the stage. He sat down on Ethan's stool, and the death glare Ethan gave him for interrupting his rehearsal was priceless! I've never heard him drop a note, but when Mike nudged him with his arse, it made him play a flat note, resulting in me letting out a snort laugh! I could pay for that later. Hopefully?

"Full house again guys, so you know the drill. Waiting staff? Listening skills on point, bar staff?"

"Yeah boss!" Levi saluted.

Mike rolled his eyes. "None of that childish behaviour. Ava?" I waved, so he knew where I was. "Watch him, would you?"

"Sure thing, Mike." I pointed at my eyes, then directed my fingers at Levi, before we both tried our best to hide our amusement.

"Ethan?" Mike turned to face him. He dropped his voice to a whisper so no one else could hear him. Ethan nodded to whatever Mike said, but by the look on his face, it wasn't good. It was like he had just seen a ghost. "Class dismissed. Get ready. See you at the end."

Levi glanced at me, and we bolted toward the stage.

"Ethan?" Levi got to him first, just as he was about to disappear into the staff room. "Mate, hold up." He grabbed his arm, turning him to face us.

The brightness in his eyes had gone and was replaced with the ghosts of the past.

"I'm sorry guys, I," He rubbed the back of his neck. "I need a moment before-" He looked at the restaurant door.

"Before what?" I asked, laying my hand on his arm. He shook his head and let the staff room door close behind him. "Ethan?"

Ethan

Don't look up. Don't look up.

My only focus tonight is the sheet music in front of me, and my fingers dancing across the keys. Yeah, I'm using sheet music tonight. The first time in years. I actually feel like I'm failing myself. If I concentrate on what I'm getting paid for, I might get through the evening without feeling like I want to drown myself in the soup Ian is cooking up in the kitchen. This is not how I wanted this evening to go. I catch Levi giving me my five-minute break wave and nod back in his direction without actually looking at him. Finishing the song, I thank the guests and move as quickly as I can toward the back of the room instead of the bar. Before I can reach the kitchen doors, a hand rests on my shoulder.

"Ethan?"

I know that voice. I know that voice oh so well. That's the voice Mike warned me about earlier. Carrie. Squeezing my eyes shut, I steady my nerves and turn around.

"Carrie."

Before I protested, she wraps me in a hug, pressing her body against mine. "Oh, Ethan, I've missed you."

"Really, that's weird."

She lets out the cutest giggle. "Why?"

"Because you broke up with me." Looking behind her, I spot Levi with his mouth open wide. He's twigged on why I wanted to be alone earlier. "What do you want Carrie?"

"I've been thinking, Ethan." She looks at her feet, then back up at me through her long lashes. "I made a mistake letting you go. I realised I was being shallow. I've changed and I still love you. Would you ever consider giving us another chance?"

This woman is something else. Yeah, she's beautiful, yeah she has curves to die for and yeah, sex with her is incredible, but do I really want her back in my life? The last thing I thought Mike was going to announce at the staff meeting was that my ex's company was in tonight. These past couple of weeks with Ava in my life?

It's been like a breath of fresh air that I almost forgot about the demon who ripped my heart out. Ava doesn't judge me for my career. She likes me for who I am. She's the one I want to be with. Not someone who says she has changed, when I know she'll fall back into her own ways with a drop of a pen.

"I don't know Carrie," *Where the fuck did that come from?* "Everything you put me through? I don't think I can do that again."

She laughs. She actually fucking laughs!

"I've changed Ethan. I'm not the same as I used to be. I love you."

"I don't think you do, Carrie. I think you like the idea of being in a relationship where you can take charge."

"Oh Ethan," she runs a manicured nail down my chest, "You know that's not true." Without warning, Carrie pulls me into her, planting her lips on mine. Her hands are in my hair and she's grinding her body against mine. For a second, I forget everything she put me through, and I kiss her back when I hear a gasp from behind me. I push Carrie off of me and look at where the sound came from, only to find Ava looking heartbroken and verging on tears.

"Ava!" I shout after her as she runs out into the street.

Carrie uses her forefinger to wipe her lips and tries to take my hand. "Oh dear. Did she like you? Shame."

I pull my hand away and turn on my VERY ex girlfriend. "You're nothing but a pain in my ass Carrie. You'll never change and you know what? I should have broken up with you well before things ended."

"Don't say that, baby. You and me, we are meant to be together."

"Carrie. Do me a favour and stay the fuck out of my life." I ran in the direction I saw Ava go, leaving Carrie to pick up her jaw from the floor.

Ian was standing in the alley with a cigarette in one hand and a cup of tea in the other.

"Which way did she go, Ian?"

Ian points toward the main square in Covent Garden. "That way."

"Thanks. Tell Mike I'm sorry." I break into a run.

"What did you do? Ethan? Ethan!"

*****

My heart is pounding in my chest as I run through the square like a huntsman trying to find Ava. I must look like a desperate idiot? An idiot in love. How could I have let that happen, and what in the fuck was Mike thinking? not telling me about Carrie attending the restaurant until the last minute. Tell me a week ahead, then I may have been able to find cover and not ruin everything I've built with Ava.

"Shit!" I scream, stopping in the middle of the street.

Turning around on the spot, I try to focus, looking for her. This was London. She could be anywhere by now. As far as messing up goes, this takes the biscuit. A shit biscuit, with no chocolate, and is made from cardboard. Typically, and as if on queue, the weather turns on me and rain pours down. Pulling my suit jacket a little tighter around me, I duck under the temple in front of St Paul's Church and reach for my phone.

Ethan - Ava, I'm so sorry. I didn't mean for that to happen.

I lean against the wall and wait for a reply. After ten minutes, I send another.

Ethan - That was Carrie, if you didn't realise already. She forced herself on me. But I guess you don't want to know that. I'm sorry.

And another...

Ethan - Mike told me her work was in tonight. I should have said something to you and Levi. I'm so sorry. I had no idea she was going to do that, let alone actually speak to me. Please forgive me. She means nothing.

Another...

Ethan - All I could think about was how wrong it was, and how much I wanted you. God, Ava, the moment I first saw you, it's been you.

Another, just to sound pathetic...

Ethan - You wanna hear it? You light me up. You inspire me. You make me feel like nothing can hurt me again. I've fallen in love with you, Ava. Please, message me back. I'm so sorry. Please.

My phone rings, and I punch the air in excitement. "Ava?"

"No! Mike! Where the fuck are you? You better get your sorry ass back here or your ass is as good as fired!"

"I'm not coming back Mike."

"The fuck you are." He sighed. "Listen Ethan, I know Carrie being there wasn't the best, but at the end of the day they are paying customers and we have a service to provide. So get your ass back here and be a man about it."

I hate to admit when Mike is right, but he is. "Wait, you said Carrie, being there wasn't the best? Are you telling me-"

"She's gone Ethan. Stormed up to Levi telling him his best friend is an asshole-"

"Can you stop calling me an asshole please?" '

"Her words, not mine. Told Levi that you're an asshole and you've missed your last chance. Then threw a pint glass in his face, which I'm guessing was meant for you, and stormed out."

A laugh escaped me. The thought of a pint soaking Levi certainly lifted my spirits.

"Where's Ava, Mike?"

"She's here. Working the bar like a champ. Why?" I fill Mike in on what happened and why I ran out on my responsibilities. "Well, shit. That sucks."

"Royally."

Mike coughed. "Listen Ethan. You've got a good heart-"

"Ugh, Mike, what's got over you?"

"Shut up. I can tell you like Ava. Hell, we all know you like each other. Be honest with her. Tell her what you told me and for the love of all that is holy. Don't mention Carrie's name. Ever again! I'll try to calm her down here as long as you get your arse back here."

Walking back into Zara Blue, I felt like a school kid who had just been disciplined for bunking off class. The waiting staff glanced in my direction, and shrugged, meaning, 'where have you been?'. I kept my head low, trying my best to ignore the glare I was receiving from Levi. Ava must have told him what she had witnessed. Removing my wet jacket, I took my seat at the piano and looked at my hands hovering over the keys. They were shaking, and I felt like shit. Nothing on this earth was going to make me feel better about breaking Ava's heart. The heart I hadn't got to experience yet. I'd blown my chance. Screwed it up beyond repair. Thank you Carrie! A mixture of emotion overwhelmed me, and I tried to steady the feeling of wanting to break down in front of a full restaurant.

Get a grip Ethan!

I let my hands go to work, playing a well rehearsed Christmas song. The audience loved it. Each table was singing and swaying along, but my mind was elsewhere. While the audience was focused on singing and drinking, I stole a glimpse toward the bar. Ava had her head down, preparing someone's cocktails and making sure she didn't look my way at all. It was clear she had been crying. Her mascara was smudged below her eyes and her beautiful face was a shadow of itself. I did that. I hurt her, just like I knew I would.

Ava

"It's over Mia, he was kissing his ex."

"Are you sure sis?"

"I know what I saw. She had her hands in his hair and," I feel a lump in my throat, "it looked like he was into it."

Tonight was like a nightmare. A nightmare I knew was coming. Ethan in the arms of the love of his life, Carrie. The way she pushed her body against his, the way she kissed him, the way he kissed her back. Why did I let myself fall for him? I should have known better. Levi was right. The only person who was going to help me crawl out of this nightmare was my sister. We had always been there for one another and we always will be.

"Ava. Everything you told me about this woman? She sounds like she was using him for her own pleasure."

"What?"

"Tell me what you heard again?"

I groan. "She said that she changed. That she's not the same and that she still loves him."

"And what did he say back?"

"He said that he doesn't think she does, and that she likes the idea of being in control, or something like that. Why?"

Mia sighed, like the all known five minute older sister that she is. "And at any point did he say. 'Oh sure, yeah Carrie, I wanna be with you too'?"

"No, but-"

"But nothing Ava! He doesn't want her."

"THEY WERE KISSING!"

"Were they kissing? Or was she kissing him? In desperation? To 'try' and get him back? Was he putting up a fight?"

"Well, he pushed her back, but that was only when he realised I was there."

I could hear Mia rubbing her temples through the phone. It was in the tone of her voice. "Are you arguing with me, or yourself? Has he text you? Called at all? Or have you ignored them like you always do?"

I pull my phone back and place Mia on speakerphone. I let out a sad sigh when I saw the photo of Ethan and I smiling at each other at the Christmas market. Yeah, I set it as my phone's wallpaper the day we got the photos back. Don't judge me! "There may have been a couple of texts."

"Let's hear them."

I read each message out loud, for the first time. Each one I read, I realise, I overreacted. Here was this perfect man, pouring his heart out in our message thread. Was it a mistake? Was he really sorry? Did Carrie force herself on him? Had I made a mistake?

"Oh my God Ava! He loves you?"

"I, er, I don't know."

"He's come out and admitted it! After everything you've told me about him, why aren't you replying?" Why wasn't I replying? "I can't"

"Why?"

"Because," I sighed in frustration. "Because I love him Mia, ok, and it's too late! I don't want to get hurt again. Ok, happy?"

"No! Of course I'm not happy. Ava, I love you, you know I do and I hate seeing you like this, or hearing you like this. If you love him and it's clear that he loves you, then what are you waiting for? And if you tell me he's still stuck on this Carrie bitch, I will disown you."

"You wouldn't dare."

"Watch me! Go to him Ava. It sounds like he's royally beating himself up about-" The sound of my phone makes Mia stop in her tracks. "What was that?"

"It's Ethan. He sent me another message."

"Open it! What does it say?"

With no hesitation, I do as my sister asks and read his text out loud.

Ethan - Ava, I don't know if you'll ever speak to me again and after what you saw tonight, I wouldn't blame you, but I just need you to know these past few weeks have been the best. You took my breath away when I first saw you, and you still do. How I got through that set was a miracle. It's killing me. I've hurt you and I would do anything for you to be

in my life again. Can we talk, please? Tonight was one massive mistake. Ethan Xx.

"Reply to him."

"What? No!"

"He just poured his heart out to you again! Reply!"

Sisters? Am I right?

"Fine!" I pressed reply and typed. "Ethan," I say as I type. As I try to think about what to say, as my mind has failed me on all accounts, another call comes through. "Hang on Mia, I've got another call," I put her on hold and answered, "Levi?"

"Ava, thank God. You've not done anything stupid."

"Why would I do something stupid, Levi?"

"Umm, I don't know, it's just, you know what nevermind. Where are you?"

"I'm at home," I let out a heavy sigh, "trying to think about how to reply to Ethan's message and failing miserably. Why?"

If Levi was now calling me, then things at their place must be bad. When a best friend calls the woman his friend wants to be with after a colossal mistake, then that friend must be in an awful place.

"I probably shouldn't be calling, but I can't sit by and watch Ethan go down the same path of depression after tonight. I don't know what to do, Ava. Please tell me you're going to message him back?"

"I don't know what to say, Levi. After what I saw? What am I supposed to say?"

I don't know how I did it, so don't cross-examine me, but somehow I let my sister into the conversion.

"Tell him you love him!"

"Who's that?" Levi asked.

"I'm Mia, Ava's twin. You must be Levi. I've heard a lot about you all."

"Bet you have! Did Ava admit to you straight away that she liked my boy, or did you figure it out by yourself as well?"

"It was pretty obvious, wasn't it?"

"Thank you guys!" I interjected. "But if we could get back to the matter at hand, please? What should I say?"

With Levi and Mia's help, I composed the message.

Ava - Ethan. I understand mistakes get made. None of us are perfect, but seeing you with your ex tonight broke my heart, because the truth is, I've fallen in love with you too...

"YEAH YOU HAVE!" Levi screamed through the phone as I read the message as I typed.

"Shut up, I'm not finished yet."

... but I think we should let what happened tonight settle between us. I want to be with you Ethan. My God, I wanted to be with you the moment we met. We can talk, but I want you to understand that I don't give out second chances easily. Christmas Eve after work? Ok?

*****

For the next two days, Ethan and I worked alongside each other as professionally as we could. Despite the heat between us, there was still the memory of his ex's lips on his. Downing a shot of vodka behind the bar, I turned and focused on my next customer. A tall man, dressed in the most hideous Christmas jumper. He sported a headband with reindeer antlers, which were decorated with tinsel. It was a fine look. Not anyone could pull this look off, but he was killing it! His friend, dressed just as colourfully and clearly excited it was Christmas, joined him.

"Nick! Grab us some more shots."

"So," I began, "more shots, is it? Will it be the same as before?" I ask Nick, who's texting on his phone.

The friend bounced back to his friends at the central table on the restaurant floor.

"If you don't mind. But," He gestured me closer and dropped his voice to a whisper, "Can you make Aidan's a double with something that will chill him the hell out?"

"Aidan?" I point toward the overexcited child, dancing with what looks like his wife to the Christmas song Ethan's currently playing, "Your friend?"

"Yeah!"

"Coming right up!" I motion to Levi to take over serving the next customer while I prepare Nick's drink order. "Tray of shots and a very special one for Aidan." I winked at Nick, sliding him the tray and watched the chaos unfold in front of me. Aidan slammed the shot back, instantly punching Nick in the arm. That's the sign of pure friendship!

The night wore on, and as more guests dispersed into the night to await the Christmas hangover, I wiped down the bar of spilt beer as I watched Ethan on stage, playing the last number of the night. The song everyone in the world sings along too, no matter how much they say they hate it. A group of women who were with Nick's crew were hugging and singing so loud they were drowning out Ethan. I caught him smiling and laughing, giving up using the microphone and letting them take over. He looked my way, and I felt myself smiling back at him, like the past few days hadn't happened and we were back to stealing glances at each other. He sang back into the microphone, keeping eye contact with me.

"All I want for Christmas," He pointed at me and winked, "is you." He raised his hand in the air. "Thank you everyone, it's been a blast! Have an amazing Christmas and get home safe."

My heart is literally beating so hard in my chest, I can hardly hear Mike talking to me about the cleanup. That was a very public display of affection.

"Shit!" I rummage for my phone to check the time. "Eleven thirty."

Enough time to freshen up before our 'chat'. Before anyone catches me, I slip into the staff room and do my best to cover the smell of beer and spirits that are currently working their way into my pores. Dropping my sister a pre Merry Christmas message, like we always do, I check myself over on the mirror and spray myself with my perfume. I don't look great, I look a mess, but it'll have to do. If he loves me like he says he does, then he'll have to suck up and deal with my choice of style for the night!

The door of the staff room opens. Ethan is standing right behind me in his tuxedo. His hair is a mess and those brown eyes are boring straight into mine.

"You look perfect." His smile makes me forget how much of a pig I feel. He looks around the staff room. "Can we, maybe, talk outside?"

"Sure." I grab my puffer jacket and sling it over my shoulders. He has his hand held out, and I instantly lace my fingers through his. The sigh he lets out makes my body come alive. As we walk through the restaurant, I can't help but spot Levi and Mike grinning like cheshire cats. Stepping out into Covent Garden Square, I'm blown away by how busy it still is. The blue lights illuminating Zara make my skin glow. It's a sight I never bore off. Mix that with the Christmas lights and decorations around the square and you feel you're in an actual seasonal movie.

Ethan guides us to where a giant reindeer is on a stand, which is also covered in fairy lights, and motions me to sit next to him.

"Ok, how do I start this?" He fidgets with his jacket sleeve and then turns to me, like the fidgeting has settled his nerves. "What happened the other night?"

"Ethan," I stop him by resting my hand on his arm. "You don't need to explain. I know it was a mistake. You've told me many times in your texts."

"I know, but I wanted to say it out loud."

"Ok." Folding my wrists across my knee, I let him continue.

"She means nothing to me. Before we met, I never thought I'd ever feel the way I do about you again. You saved me Ava, literally saved me from a spiral of depression. When she forced herself on me," He actually cringed at the memory, "I almost lost control, but then I remembered. She's vile. Capable of using people to her own advantage. She'll never change and I know now that I wasted too much of my life with her."

"How is this helping in your case, Ethan?"

"What I'm trying to say is, I don't want anyone else Ava. All I want is you."

"Is that why you ended the night on that song?" I nudge him as he turns a shade of pink. "It was cute."

A couple dance in the street in front of us. The woman loses her footing, but the man catches her before she hits the ground. They both fall about laughing.

"That's what I want," I say, as I scoot closer to Ethan, resting my head on his shoulder. "To be silly with each other and not give a damn who's watching."

"Are you saying what I think you're saying?"
Resting a hand on Ethan's knee, I turn to face him. "You said that when you first saw me, I took your breath away?"

"You still do."

"Well," I play with the fabric of his trousers, running my finger across his leg, which awards me with a very sexy inhale. "I'd be lying if I didn't say you had the same effect on me."

A smile spreads across his face while he plays with a strand of my hair, gently tucking it behind my ear before pulling me close to him as the bells of St Paul's Church ring on Christmas Day.

"I love you so much Ava."

"Love you back Ethan."

THE END

SELFRIDGES
Amy C. Beckinsale
©AmyCBeckinsale2022

CHAPTER ONE

"Must hurry. Must hurry."

Running as fast as I could in my five inch red heels, I dodged fellow shoppers who had also left Christmas shopping until the last minute. Sensing my opportunity, as a woman with a pram took a right-hand turn, I made one last push to get into the world famous Selfridges on Oxford Street.

"Please don't be closed."

The wooden revolving door was still turning. I was in luck!

YES!

Stepping into the entrance of the store, I breathed a sigh of relief, coughing seconds later when the overwhelming scent of perfume caught the back of my throat. Shoppers looked at me, not in concern, but in a snooty uptight 'How dare you cough in a prestige department store' kind of way. Now I had the job of trying to find my little sister the necklace she had been hinting about since August! How hard could it be? Right? All I had to do was find the relevant department, pray that it had not sold out, pay for the necklace, then catch the train back to the family home in Guildford.

Taking the lift to the fourth floor, I ran toward the jewellery displays, tapping along the pristine glass with my fresh Christmas themed manicured nails. I stopped tapping when I found what I sought. There it was, in all its glory. A baby pink unicorn necklace, with matching coloured rainbows to make any eleven-year-old girls' Christmas. I let out a squeal. I was going to make Violet's Christmas wish come true!

"Excuse me?" I asked an assistant. "Could I please see this necklace?"

"Certainly, madam." The assistant placed the necklace in my hand.

"So pretty. Violet will love it." I passed it back. "I'll take it, thank you."

"Very good, madam." She began ringing up the transaction. "Would you like it gift wrapped? For an extra five pounds, you get a beautiful lace bag."

"Even more perfect. Thank you."

The assistant worked her skilled magic, wrapping the jewellery box in light purple paper, which sparkled when it caught the light. She then produced a silk white ribbon, finishing it with an expert bow, before placing the box safely in the lace bag. It was beautiful.

"And presto, fit for a princess."

*****

Christmas present in hand, I had time to pick up a cold drink before I decided on a taxi rather than catching the underground to Waterloo Station. I watched the city lights fly by as the car worked its way through the city. Driving over Westminster bridge, I took a photo of the Christmas lights over the River Thames, posting it on my social media sites with a supporting message showing off that I had finished work for the year. My friends in retail would soon be slating my ass for such a comment, since they had to work throughout the holidays. A chore I did not envy. I was too pumped. I'd got my little sister's present and was now on my way home. All I could think about was seeing Violet and my parents.

Many siblings had different relationships, but mine and Violet's? Ours was solid, built on love and trust. I was only twelve when Violet was born and from the first moment I held my baby sister, I felt an overpowering love. I would do anything for Violet and would summon the demons from hell if anyone hurt her.

*****

The taxi pulled into the drop off point. Paying the driver, I made my way into the main section of the station and joined other travellers looking up at the departure board.

Bugger!

The train to Guildford was displayed as delayed.

Of all the days?

I turned on my heel in a huff, ready to mouth off about the British rail service, when I walked flat into a tall man standing behind me, spilling his coffee all over his suit jacket.

"For the love of_" He shook his hands to rid them of coffee.

"Oh, my goodness. I am so sorry. Let me help." I looked up to the man I decided to give a coffee shower to. "That was entirely my, Owen?"

"Huh?"

"You're Owen Turner." I found myself smiling. "God, it's been years."

"What now?"

"Ruby, Ruby Musgrave." I pointed to herself. "We were at school together in Guildford before your family moved to the city."

A smile began to form on his face as a faint memory began to bloom.

"English and French, if I'm not wrong?"

"Yes!"

He clapped his hands together, since the coffee cup was lying on the floor, rejected. "How are you? Apart from soaking me in coffee."

"I'm good, just waiting for my delayed train home. Again!"

'Delayed? On Christmas Eve? What are the odds?" He glanced around, then picked up the empty cup. "Listen, I've got a bit of time before my mate gets in from Farnham. Seeing as it's probably the same train, how about we grab another coffee?"

I found myself getting lost in his dark brown eyes, again, just like I used to in school. The number of times the tutor would ask me a question about the subject and I'd have to face the embarrassment of asking them to repeat themselves because I was too busy admiring Owen, was sky high.

"Sure."

*****

Placing my bags behind my feet, I sat and waited for my childhood friend, from way back when, to return with our drinks. Of all the places and of all the days, the last thing I expected was to run into a friend, let alone soak him in coffee!

During my school years, Owen and I weren't that close. We knew one another existed, but it wasn't until the last few months before his family moved into the city that our friendship grew. After he left, there was the promise to keep in touch, but that wore thin as life took over and our paths to higher education and careers took the main priority. And now? Now I knew that after this brief coffee date, I probably wouldn't see him again after we parted ways once more.

"Large soy hazelnut latte with cream?" Owen said, reading my order from the side of the cup. He placed my coffee down. "Hell of an order." He sat next to me. Closely. "Are you planning on staying awake for a week?"

"When you have a little sister who gets excited about Christmas as she does, you need all the caffeine you can get."

"Sounds like my pain in the ass brother. You gotta love them, though, right?" Owen took a sip of his second latte. "So tell me, what are you up to these days?"

I opened up, easily, and began telling him how I'd studied media at college, and how I landed work experience within the local radio station in my hometown, resulting in an interview with the station master for a full-time position. Owen didn't interrupt once. He just listened, unlike some other friends who are just interested in themselves.

I knew I had to work hard to stay in the music industry, and it paid off. My boss, who travelled to London for multiple meetings, mentioned how good I was at my job and I soon found that I had attracted their attention. I hardly believed my luck when I was invited for a meeting of my own, to work for one of the biggest radio stations in the city. Especially at such a young age.

"Now I have the chance to be an actual producer, and not just the assistant."

"That's incredible Ruby. You must be ecstatic?"

"It's going to be hard work, but it'll be so worth it. What about you?"

"Well, I went to college and uni in London, and now I work for a software company in Liverpool Street"

"Software?"

"Software, computers, IT_" I nodded in

understanding. "But, my mate is launching his own company so we're working on our own programmes. Aidan's already got some apps out on the market already."

"Ahh, the dream of being your own boss."

"Absolutely. Can't wait to branch out on our own, and Aidan comes from a strong line of businessmen, so he'll kick this out of the park."

Talk soon changed to how our families were doing, which friends we'd stayed in touch with since school and if either of us had heard the news that one friend had become a reality star in Canada by becoming a contestant on The Bachelorette! Laughter, jokes, and reminiscing over times gone by. It was like no time had passed since the last time we hung out, but when I reached out and touched Owen's hand as I smiled at a story she was telling, I felt a spark of electricity between us. I pulled back, feeling embarrassed but also excited.

"Sorry."

Owen took hold of my hand again. "Don't be."

Meeting his dark eyes, I smiled, interlinking her fingers with his. "Owen, I_"

THIS IS THE FINAL ANNOUNCEMENT FOR THE DELAYED TRAIN CALLING AT GUILDFORD. THE TRAIN IS ABOUT TO DEPART FROM PLATFORM FOUR.

"Shit!" Scraping the chair across the pristine white floor resulting in an ear torturing squeal, I grabbed my bags. "I'm sorry, I_I have to go. It's been amazing to catch up with you Owen. I wish we had more time, but. I'm so sorry. I gotta go."

I didn't look back, as much as I wanted to, running down the stairs to get to the platform, leaving Owen speechless and in bewilderment. That spark would be hard to forget.

"Nice to see you again, Ruby." I heard from behind me.

Boarding the train seconds before the doors closed, I walked down the carriage trying to find an empty seat, eventually finding one at the far end, next to a middle-aged woman.

"Excuse me, is this seat taken?" I pointed at the vacant space.

"No, my dear, please," the woman tapped the seat. "join me."

"Thank you."

Collapsing, as the train slowly pulled away from the station, a sense of relief after yet another sprint washed over me. Running is not my forte and I have no intention in making it a New Year's resolution! Thank the lord for the next two weeks off, I'm gonna need the rest after taking part in what felt like a marathon!

From the noise of a group at a table seat, toasting gin and tonic from cans, the journey wasn't going to be a quiet one. They were clearly celebrating more than Christmas and when they popped open another can each, it was only going to get louder. I closed my eyes and placed my earphones in choosing my eighties playlist. Modern music had delivered some impressive bands, but my secret love was and always will be the era of shell suits and big hair! Listening to The Clash, my mind began to wander. To Owen Turner. He'd changed so much since school, his height being a big change. He must have had a growth spurt after his family moved away, because he was a lot taller than when I saw him last. One thing that hadn't changed was his smile. Every time I saw it, I always found myself smiling back. Which, coincidentally, was how our friendship began. It was in school. He smiled. I smiled. Our eyes met. He smiled more. I giggled. He frowned in confusion. I snorted and laughed in embarrassment. He approached me to see if I was ok. I smiled again and the rest, as they say, is history.

The journey went by in a breeze, and before long, the conductor announced the arrival in Guildford. Reaching for my bags and pulling my ear phones out, placing them safely in my jacket pocket, I wished my fellow passenger goodbye and stepped onto the platform. The chill made the hair on the back of my neck rise. Pulling my coat around me a little tighter and shaking it off, I practically skipped through the station, swinging my bags in delight. I'd made it home for the holidays, I'd reconnected with an old school friend (despite actually getting his number) and was now about to make my little sister's Christmas.

"Shit!"

Dropping to the floor, I rummaged through my shopping. Gifts, belongings, clothes went everywhere but panic struck.

"No, no, no, no, no" I spun around and watched the train pull away. "NO! This can not be happening?"

It was happening. I'd lost the only gift I was determined to get. The most important and the most special. That beautiful lace bag was gone. The bag, containing Violet's dream gift. On a destination to butt fuck wherever!

"How can I be such an idiot?" A lightbulb lit. "WAIT! THAT'S IT!"

I opened my phone, typing as fast as I could to find the train and where its final destination was. Find the contact details for the company, get in contact and ask them to conduct a military search to recover the gift. Problem solved. Christmas saved.

"Fuck!"

What's the point? Someone would have stolen it by now. I locked my phone, placing it in my pocket before holding my head in my hands and screaming internally. All that running around London and I still managed to cock up. I let out a long groan and picked up my belongings, swearing to myself under my breath. An old woman walked pastme and gave me a dirty look. She must have heard my outburst.

"Sorry." I shuffled my belongings back into my bag and made my way to the taxi rank. All the way, thinking about how I was going to break the news to Violet about why her big sister hadn't bought her a present.

CHAPTER TWO

"Six forty-five, love."

I glanced up to find the taxi driver looking back at me in the rear-view mirror. "Umm, yeah, sure. Card ok?"

"Whatever's easiest."

Tapping my card on the contactless pad, I wished the driver a Merry Christmas, got out, and stared at the family home. The lights outside were once again spectacular. Dad had an artistic flare, colour coordinating the lights to match the tone of the building. It was warm, inviting and BRIGHT! Really bright. Brighter than last year.

I greeted a reindeer made of grapevine as I stepped closer to the front door. "Evening Vixen."

My nerves were shot. I had no idea how to break the news to my little sister. Before unlocking the door, I peered into the living room window and sighed, seeing Violet sat crossed legged in front of the television enjoying a Christmas variety show with our parents. She looked so happy and full of excitement.

"You can do this Ruby, you can do this." I turned the key in the lock, and instantly heard the bark of the family dog, Millie. The border collie jumped up. Her tail wagged so much, it was a blur.

"Hey girl. You miss me?" I scratched behind Millie's soft ears. Her sweet spot. "Yes, you did. Yes, you did." Dumping my bags on the stairs, I called out for life. "Hello?"

Violet appeared instantly at the sound of my voice. "Ruby!" She threw her arms around me. "You're finally here."

"Eventually. I'm sorry I'm late. My train was delayed. You better not have started our favourite movie without me?"

"We have it lined up and ready."

"Good girl."

Throwing my coat over the bannister, I followed my sister into the living room.

"Hi parents." Mum and Dad were up and hugging the life out of me before insisting I sit my ass down and tell them all about work and life in the city. I updated them, answering every question they sent my way, grateful to avoid the unknown elephant in the room. My sister's present.

"I know I say it every time you come home, my Ruby jewel," Dad tapped my knee. "But I am so proud of what you have achieved,"

"Thanks Dad," I laid my hand over his and gave it a squeeze. "Now, how about that movie?" I moved to the floor, sitting next to my sister. Both of us reached for a cushion to hug. "You know it's not Christmas until we watch it,"

*****

Two hours later, Violet was fast asleep. Her head leaning on my arm gently snoring.

"Vi? Movies over,"

"Hmmm?"

"And that's bedtime," Mum said, picking her youngest daughter up, but groaned. "Oh, she's getting bigger."

"Let me Mum, you've clearly been working to your bones today."

"Thank you, darling."

Easily lifting her, I adjusted my hold to make sure her head was supported. All that time in the company gym had paid off. I kissed Mum's cheek and smiled at her dad, also asleep, but still hugging his Christmas Eve brandy.

"Night Mum."

"Good night jewel."

*****

Climbing the stairs, I opened Violet's door with my foot and placed her on her bed. Pulling the covers up, I made sure she was tucked in and then stroked her hair.

"Violet, there's something I have to tell you, and I don't know where to even start." All around her room, unicorn toys and decor looked back at me like they were judging my mistake. I closed my eyes and shook my head. "God, I am the worst sister ever. I can't even bring a bag home without losing it. Sis, I'm sorry, I really am, but that necklace you_"

"Ruby?" Mum called.

Interrupted mid confession. Thanks Mum. I took one more look at my sleeping sister.

"I suppose I'll just have to break the news tomorrow. Good night sis."   I closed her bedroom door and walked down the stairs. "Yeah Mum? What's up?"

Mum pointed at the front door. "You have a visitor."

"Now?" I checked the time on my phone. "It's almost eleven at night."

Opening the door, I couldn't believe who I saw.

"Do you have any idea how long it took me to track you down?" Owen said. The fresh falling snow laid on his shoulders, and that heartbreaking smile spread across his handsome face. Was I dreaming?

"Owen?" I turned around to see the smug grin on Mum's face. "What are you doing here? And at this hour?"

"Well, when you ran off in a state of panic, you forgot something." He produced the white lace bag. "I believe this is yours?"

I gasped, then snatched it out of his hand, frantically looking inside. "Oh my God!"

"I guessed it must have been important to you, so instead of going out for drinks with Aidan and some pals from work, I borrowed a mate's car and, well, here I am."

Tears filled behind my eyes. "Owen, you have no idea how much this means to me. How much it will mean to Violet?" Without thinking, I flung my arms around him, holding him close. "Thank you, thank you so much."

Owen held me close. His hands rubbing my back. "Hey, what's with the tears?"

I wiped the tears from my eyes. "I'm sorry. It's just this gift is going to make my little sister so happy and when I thought I'd lost it, I couldn't believe how much I messed up. Then I had to deal with the fact that I had to tell her I hadn't bought her a present and she's been dropping hints about this necklace since August. And then_"

"Whoa, whoa, relax. I get it, trust me." He gently

pushed some hair out of my eyes and held the side of my head. "You don't have to worry about upsetting your sister now and I'm sure, if she's anything like you, she would have completely understood."

I placed my hand over his. There was that spark again.

"You think so?"

"I know so. And as an elder brother who watches over his own little brother, I also know how much pressure we put on ourselves to make sure they are never upset or sad. Tom may be a royal pain in my ass from time to time, but it doesn't mean I wouldn't drop the world for him. So believe me, I understand what you're feeling."

Looking down at the pretty bag again, I smiled. "This means so much Owen, I, wait! You're missing a party? For me?"

"There will be other parties."

"But you were waiting for your friend. Was he ok about you ditching him?"

"He'll be fine. Besides this way, I get to see you twice in one day. Unexpected, of course."

An awkward giggle escaped me. "Can't complain there." I looked up at him and lost myself in those eyes again.

"So, umm, I should probably get back, it's late, and the weather doesn't look like it's going to be on my side for much longer however," Owen rummaged in his bag, producing a business card and gave it to her. "When you're back in the city, call me, ok?"

I took the card with no hesitation, which comprised Owen's personal and work contact details.

"Absolutely." I tucked it into the back pocket of my jeans.

Owen smiled. That smile. The one I'd admired in school. That I still admire. *Help me Jesus*!

"Merry Christmas, Ruby."

"Merry Christmas, Owen."

CHAPTER THREE

Closing the door, I could already feel my parents' smug faces watching me. Turning around, there they were. Two sets of eyebrows raised. A slight head tilt to their left and smiles that asked the question. 'Who was that?'

"Before you ask." I went into the living room and put Violet's present under the tree. "That was a friend. Nothing else, so don't go getting all excited and proclaiming it was a Christmas romance miracle."

"Well," Mum placed a hand on her hip. "Was it though?"

"Stop it, Mum."

"What made him drive all the way from London, then?"

Insert long groan here. Here we go. Question time.

"I got that necklace for Violet, you know, the one she's been going on about?" They both nodded. They knew about the necklace. I wasn't the only one Violet had nagged. "Owen's an old friend from school."
Dad clapped his hands together. "Turner! Owen Turner? That's where I recognised him from. His family used to live in the street along from us."

"Roy." Mum smacked his stomach. "Hush yourself, you'll wake Vi."

"Sorry Jill."

"Anyway," I continued. "I ran into Owen at Waterloo when my train was delayed. He got talking over a coffee about old times and time slipped away. Almost missed my train, and it wasn't until I got here that I realised I'd misplaced Violet's gift."

Mum held her hands over her heart. Here it comes.

"And he travelled all this way to give it back? Ruby, sweetheart." She engulfed me in a mum hug. "He must really like you. What are you going to do about it?"

"What do you mean, what am I going to do about it? I thanked him and wished him and his family a Merry Christmas."

"Come on, jewel." Dad placed an arm around my shoulders. "Don't hide it. We all saw what he gave you."

Before I had time to resist, Dad stole the business card from my back pocket and was reading it aloud.

"DAD!"

"Owen Turner. Senior IT Technician. Liverpool St, London." He made an impressive whistle sound. "Senior, eh? Oh look, and all his contact details."

"Let's see?"

Mum snatched the card out of my dad's hands. I was not going to win this. The problem of being five foot four with tall parents. "Come on, guys."

"Plus email, personal and business."

I reached up and stole the card back. "I love you guys, but seriously? Boundaries."

"Ruby, you know very well your dad and I don't know the meaning of the word."

"Clearly!" I placed the card in the back of my plastic phone case. That way, there was no way they could get near it there.

I was about to wish my nosy parents goodnight and try to forget the embarrassment they always manage to cause when the doorbell sounded again. Mum and Dad shared a look.

Oh, god, no!

This time, Dad was the one to answer. He opened the door to a snow covered Owen.

"Hi, again. I'm sorry to disturb you on Christmas Eve."

"Good heavens lad, it's blowing a blizzard, don't stand out there in the cold."

"Thank you so much. As soon as it's clear enough to drive, I'll be out of your hair."

"You'll stay for as long as needed lad, we'll take good care of you. Won't we jewel?"

Thank you Dad!

His teasing remarks made my face burn. I could feel the heat rising like a kettle ready to explode. I may have told my parents Owen, and I were only friends, but now it was clear as day. I liked this guy. I've always liked him and I probably always will and they knew it. Mum, being the sensible one of my parents, took my embarrassment of a state as a hint.

"Why don't we get you snuggled up by the fire? Get

that chill off while Ruby pops the kettle on." She guided Owen by the elbow into our seasonal living room, rubbing his arms to keep him warm. More likely trying to get an idea if he was in good shape by grabbing a feel of a bicep. I take it back, Mum is worse than Dad. "Ruby? Kettle?"

"There really is no need, I'll be gone before you know it."

"But in the meantime, you can enjoy a nice hot mug of tea."

Owen tried to hide his amusement at my parents over the top, welcome to our house and take our daughter on a date, hint and glanced my way. He gave me a gentle smile which read. 'Thank you. I'm sorry. I didn't mean to impose, but I'm also really glad I get to see you again'.

"Did you want tea, Owen?" I asked, as he settled down on the sofa. "Or something else? Coffee? Hot chocolate? They have everything here."

"You know what would be a mighty fine choice." Dad lent on his elbows, sitting opposite Owen. "Another glass of brandy. What do you say Owen? Won't you join me?"

Owen's eyes darted between Dad, myself, Mum, and back to me again. "I suppose a small one couldn't hurt? Wouldn't be Christmas Eve if a little alcohol wasn't poured."

"That's a good lad!" Slapping his thighs, Dad made a B-Line for the drinks cabinet. "It's an old family tradition," He said as he poured the drinks. "We toast on Christmas Day by drinking and thanking our lucky stars we get to spend the holiday together."

Owen gratefully accepted his drink, breathing in the liquor's fragrance. "Isn't that more of a New Year's thing?"

"We do it for both." Dad sat back down, not offering anyone else a drink. Mum and I exchanged a look, got the hint and parked our backsides down. "Gives us another excuse to break out the good stuff again. Give it a whirl."

Taking a sip, as Dad watched him drink, Owen's eyes lit up.

"Shitting hell, that's good. What brand is it?"

That was it. Dad had well and truly dug his paws in,

and if Dad had anything to do with it, Owen wasn't going anywhere, not at least until tomorrow afternoon.

Leaving the two men to talk over brandy, I slipped out to the kitchen to make myself and Mum a hot chocolate. Before I rounded the corner, I stole a peek at Owen. He wore that smile that made my heart bounce, and when he caught me staring at him, it grew even more.

SHIT!

I ducked out as quickly as I could to save myself even more embarrassment. Turning on the stove, to heat the milk, I drew the blinds up. The snow had eased a bit and the garden, from where the kitchen window looked out, was like a scene out of a movie. More Christmas lights reflected from the fresh snow. Taking my phone out of my pocket, I snapped a photo, loading it on my social media pages for my friends to see. A hand lay on my shoulder, and the movement made me jump. Spinning around, I almost dropped my phone in the milk, but as quickly as I spun, my reflexes triggered and I caught it just before it drove into the warm milk.

"Crap, I'm sorry. I didn't mean to startle you." Owen said, brandy glass in hand and his other hand up in defence. "Did you save it?"

"Huh?"

"Your phone." He pointed to the milk. "Did you get it before it?"

"Oh, uh, yeah. How's the brandy?"

Owen looked at the glass in his hand. "Your Dad knows his drink. He gave me the name of the place he picked it up. Think Aidan will appreciate it as well." He swigged the past of the liquid and placed his glass down. "So, I should be making my way back. Looks like the snow has calmed down enough to make it back to London."

I'm not going to lie. The thought of Owen leaving cut me deep. I don't know why I'd thought he'd stay for Christmas, he has a family of his own and friends waiting for him back in the city. That didn't stop me from feeling disappointed, though.

"Sure." I turned, making an excuse to stir the milk and to hide my let down face. "Of course."

"Ruby?"

He lay both of his hands on both of my shoulders and leaned close. So close, I could smell his cologne and the brandy still lingering on his breath. Any closer and his body would be pressed up against mine. I closed my eyes, imagining what that feeling would be like. To press myself against him. To enjoy the pressure of his body.

"Tell me what's going on in that beautiful mind of yours." He said, watching my reflection in the window. *What did he just say? Did he just call me beautiful? Does he know I'm imagining what he looks like under his clothes?*

Before I knew it, Owen spun me around to face him. His hands are now on my waist. Gripping to the fabric of my top, he pulled me closer and pressed his lips against my own. Without hesitation, my arms reached for him, circling his neck, as I allowed him to deepen the kiss. The mixture of liquor and the heat between us was like a feeling I had never experienced, and I loved it. The way his hand roamed up and down my body made my back arch, pushing myself even closer, resulting in a low and very sexy groan to escape him. I felt a sensation on my back, a weird sensation.

A playful giggle escaped me. "Ahh, not too rough."

"That wasn't me." He said, in between kisses.

I felt it again and then it hit me. "The milk!"

Spinning me out of danger, Owen grabbed a nearby cloth and pulled the pan off the hob, turning down the heat. He lent down to sniff and scrunched up his face

"Yeah, you're not gonna want to drink that."

He threw it down the sink. The smell of burnt milk wafted into the air, making him complain in a not so sexy groan. I covered my mouth with my hand as a laugh escaped me.

"Perhaps I should just stick to herbal tea tonight."

He turned and matched my laughter, pulling me close again.

"Have you got a habit of burning milk? Or is this a 'caught up in the moment and got distracted' kind of thing?" He asked, planting another kiss on me, which I gratefully accepted.

"I wasn't the one making the distraction. That was all you." I breathed in, deeply, remembering why he had joined me in the kitchen.. "Do you really have to go? Wouldn't it be safer to drive back in daylight?"

He sighed. At the same time running a hand through my hair. I leaned into his touch as he said the words I knew were coming, but didn't want to hear.

"I really need to be getting back, as much as I would like to stay for a while longer." Pulling away from me, he readjusted his clothing that I appeared to have misshapen'd. "My parents are expecting me to get to theirs in the morning."

"Oh, ok." Turning my back on him, trying to hide my disappointment once more.

"Ruby." Engulfing me in his arms, I melted into him, enjoying his warmth. His chest pressed hard against my back. "After the traditional Christmas celebrations," He kissed my neck, my eyes closed, wanting to relish the feeling of his lips on my skin once more. "I'm all yours."

"Is that a promise?"

"Come back to London for New Year's and I'll prove it to you."

CHAPTER FOUR

Sinking into my childhood single bed, dressed in classic My Little Pony sheets (Thank you Mum!), I reached for my phone to set the alarm. Nice and early. An hour ago I thought Christmas was ruined by my stupidity, but a knight in shining armour saved the day. I still couldn't believe Owen had changed his plans for me. Driving all this way when he was meant to be meeting friends for drinks to save my ass. He was always kind when we were in school. Sticking up for the quiet kids and defending the nerds who were being picked on, but I never thought he would do what he did tonight. I don't even know I could even begin to repay him. Well, there is one way, but I can't think like that right now. He's on his way back to London! I opened a new message and typed his number into the 'add new contact' box.

RUBY - I still can't believe what you did this evening. Thank you. Drive safe. Text me when you're back, so I don't worry. Ruby Xx

I stared at the message until it announced that it had been delivered. Happy, I placed it back on the nightstand, where I would stare at the screen until I saw someone typing, knowing a reply was going to be announced within seconds. But Owen was driving. In the snow. On the motorway. Great! Now I'm going to have panic attacks about his safety until I hear from him. Moisturising my hands and face, I switched the light off and tried to sleep. There was one problem, though. As soon as I was plunged into darkness and closed my eyes, my mind thought of how he held me close as he kissed me. The taste of brandy on his lips and his scent which made the air on my body stand on end. Damn. There was no way I was going to sleep. I was too charged up.

*****

"Merry Christmas Ruby jewel!"

What in the actual hell?
"Wakey, wakey sleepy head."
Not now Dad.
"Don't tell me you're stuck to the bed again, jewel?"
Oh, God, no.
"You know what that means."

Dad pulled the duvet back, and I knew what was coming. Something he did when I was a teenager. When I refused to get my backside out of the warm bed. A wet flannel to the face, and here it came. I let out a scream as the cold, wet fabric contacted my face. Dreams turned into laughter.

"DAD! Come on! I'm not a kid anymore! Stop it." I jumped up out of bed. His point had been made. "Ok, ok, I'm up, I'm up."

"Still works like a charm."

"Oh, yeah?" I challenged him. I looked back at my bed.

"Don't you dare."

"Watch me."

We stared at each other until I made the first move. I was so close to comfort again, but Dad had a trick up his sleeve. In record speed, he stole my duvet.

"HA!" He threw the duvet over the bannister landing in the hallway downstairs with a really pathetic sound. Doof. "What's the point of a bed if there is no duvet?

I applauded him, slowly. Patronising. "Good move, Dad. But you've made a mistake."

"Oh, yeah?" He mocked. "And what is that?"

I grabbed my phone and ran out of my teenage room. Flying down the stairs, I shouted back. "That I can easily make the sofa a makeshift bed!"

"Touche."

Picking up my duvet which got caught in my footing, making me almost face-plant the floor, I drove onto the sofa. I laughed as Dad lent on the doorframe of the living room shaking his head. He'd given up. What he didn't realise was that his youngest daughter would be following in my footsteps before too long and pulling the same devious tricks as I am now.

"I give up!" He threw his hands in the air and joined Mum in the kitchen, who was already making a start on

Christmas dinner.

Feeling smug that I had once again won the daughter/father play fight, I checked my phone. One missed call and three texts.

I opened the phone to find Owen's name at the top of the screen before turning my attention to the texts.

Owen - Hi, I'm guessing you must be asleep, but I promised to let you know when I got back. Well, I'm back. Drive was ok.

Owen - Morning beautiful. Merry Christmas. I'm on my way to my parents. I hope the present goes down well with your sister.

Owen - So my brother wants to know all about you already, but I want to keep you to myself. He's pissing me off, just like I told you he does. Is it bad that I want to punch my sibling on Christmas Day?

I laughed and hit reply.

Ruby - Punching your little brother on Christmas morning isn't what I would call 'festive'. LOL. He can't be THAT bad? Xx

Owen - When you eventually meet him, you'll want to hit him too, believe me! How did you sleep? Xx

Ruby - Hmm, sleep. Yeah, someone was racing through my mind all night. Made it hard to switch off. If you know what I mean?

Owen - That person would say sorry, but he's not ;)

"Ruby, sweetheart. Coffee?" Mum shouted, breaking my trail of thought.

"Yes, please Mum. Thanks."

I hit reply again when Violet jumped on me, snuggling down so she looked like a cat, curled up next to me. She was wearing her unicorn pyjamas and had already mastered the high bun look. Finishing the look with slipper boots that matched the purple and pink of her sleep wear.

"Who are you texting?"

She tried to steal my phone. I avoided her little hands by holding the phone up high. "No one you know."

Her eyes lit up. "Is it a boy?" Energy, that I'm sure she had stored away somewhere, exploded out of her. She moved as quick as a ninja and managed to snatch my phone out of my hands. Unlocked. I forget that she's older than she looks and knows about boyfriends. Is Owen my boyfriend now? That's one for another time. Right now, I have a little sister who is going to grill me for the rest of the holidays.

"Owen Turner." She reads the name at the top of our thread. "Why's he not sorry you didn't sleep?"

Mum returned, right, at, the, wrong, moment?

"You didn't sleep, jewel?" She passed me my coffee.
Oh, no!

"Is it because Owen was here until late into the night?" Mum winked at me. "I saw the pair of you getting cosy in the kitchen."
FACEPALM TO THE FACE.

"You snogged a boy?" Violet said, using a pitch only dogs should be able to hear. "Yuck!" She scrunched her face up in disgust.

"Ok, yes! Owen and I kissed. Can we leave it there, please?" I pulled the duvet over my head when I felt the heat reaching my cheeks. That, however, did not stop Mum and Violet from wanting more information.

"So, are you going to see him again?" Mum asked, clearly not getting the hint.

There was no point in hiding. Resorted back to being a teenager, I pushed the duvet back down and pouted. "Yes, probably. He actually invited me out for New Year."

"In the city?" Violet tried to steal my phone again, since she thought I was distracted.

Nice try, sis.

"Yes, in the city." This conversation was not going to end, but Dad came to the rescue.

"Christmas breakfast is ready! First come, first

served!"

Yes! Breakfast. Thank you Dad.

Breakfast in this house was usually like any other. Cereal, toast. Coffee, tea. The occasional bagel. But on Christmas Day? We went all out! Bacon, sausage, hash browns, beans, scrambled egg or poached, tomatoes, button mushrooms and toast. It was divine and a treat we looked forward to when Dad made the announcement not to overfill the night before. We would be set until Christmas dinner.

Entering the kitchen, I looked at the spot where Owen and I kissed. Where he ran his hands up and down my body. Where he made my body shudder in excitement at feeling his own reaction to mine. I breathed in and felt my exhale quiver as my legs began to tingle at the memory. God, I want that man so badly. I want to see him lying on my bed, back in London, naked and ready for me. I bit my lower lip in anticipation.

"You ok Ruby?" My Mum said, filling her plate with food.

"Uh, yeah, yeah I'm good." *I need an excuse.* "I just need to pee, be right back. Save me some bacon."

I ran up the stairs just as I heard Dad shouting.

"Can't promise that."

Locking the bathroom door, I lent on the edge of the sink looking at myself in the mirror. The thought of Owen lying on my bed, naked and kissing me, made my body come alive with fire. I could imagine him making love to me until I cried out his name in ecstasy. I opened my phone and called him. I had to hear this voice. He answered in seconds.

"Hey beautiful_"

"Tell me what you'd do to me," I interrupted him.

"Like what?"

"If we were together, alone, what would you do to me? Tell me."

He let out a low groan. He knew where I wanted to take this.

"Well, I suppose I'd begin by caressing every part of you. Watch you as my hands travel across your body. From your breasts down_"

"How far down?" I slipped a hand into my underwear.

"To where I imagine you are right now."

I sucked in a moan, biting my lip as I rocked against my own hand. "What else?"

"I'd follow the trail with my mouth, enjoy the taste of you and make you want to scream even before I've let you."

"Then?"

"Then, when I think you'll shout at me if I don't do what I know you want, I'd slip into you and fuck you until you scream."

I moan at his words as my body shakes in response to what I know is another promise. My body tightens and my breath staggers as I enjoy my climax. Letting out a sigh of contentment, I can hear Owen grinning through the phone.

"Next time you decide you want to do that, we're using face time. Oh, and by the way." He drops his voice to a whisper. "You have no idea how much I want you right now."

I let out a giggle. "Well, when I meet you for New Year, I'll just have to make it up to you."

"Is that a promise?"

"It's a certainty."

CHAPTER FIVE

An unexpected activity and breakfast done, the family gathered in the living room, showered and dressed to exchange gifts. Another rule in this house is that presents had to wait until we were fed, washed and dressed. Mainly so Mum could take photos of us all in our finery. I never understood why we had to get dressed up in sparkles, full makeup, and heels just to sit in our own living room, slowly getting royally pissed as the day went on. To the point where we were all falling asleep watching the Christmas specials of our favourite tv programmes. But if it was what Mum wanted, who was I to argue with her? When I'm a mum, I can set the rules. PJ's and slippers all day! Until then, I'd do as I was asked.

"This one's for you Daddy." Violet passed Dad a wrapped gift which had racing cars on it. "Hope you like it." She sat back on her heels, bouncing up and down in excitement as Dad painfully opened the present.

"Come on Roy, just bloody rip it."

"I will open it at my own pace, thank you dear." He dismissed the racing car paper and smiled. "Awe, Vi, this is brilliant. Thank you."

"What did you get?" Mum asked, already knowing what it was since she helped Violet buy the present.

"It's a racing day at Silverstone." He opened the experience day box and let out a whistle. "Says I can drive an Aston Martin and a Ferrari. Thank you Violet." He lent across to give my baby sister a big hug.

"Ruby next, Mum!" Violet screamed in excitement. "The black box!"

"Ok sweetie." Mum reached for the large black box that I hadn't noticed sitting under the tree. "We all put a lot of work into this, but we hope you'll love it and make some happy memories."

Ok, so now I'm confused. What had they done? I took the box from Mum. Dad was grinning like a cheshire cat at me, and Violet looked like she was about to burst in excitement.

"What have you guys done?"

I'll admit, I was feeling nervous. With the way they were all looking at me, I had a feeling they had done something above and beyond. I pulled the red ribboned bow. The fabric fell elegantly around me, and Violet displayed her ninja skills once more, grabbing the ribbon and making me an Alice band. The sides of the box fell open, and I gasped at what I saw.

"You're kidding me? How did you manage to afford_?" Inside the box was a pair of keys and the deeds to a one-bedroom flat in London. "I can't believe this!"

"Well, believe it." Dad threw his arm around me as I studied the box's content again. "Remember when your late uncle passed away when you were young and we said he had left us some money?"

"Yeah, but what has this got to do with me?"

"From the sale of his estate and the inheritance, it worked out to be quite a substantial amount." Dad said, enjoying another glass of brandy. "One of his instructions was to set you up in your own place. To get you on the property ladder."

A tear escaped me and the sound of a camera went off. Mum was capturing the moment.

"The same goes for Violet." Mum put the camera down and engulfed my sister. "We've set a lump sum aside to do the same for her."

"Seriously!" Violet's excitement hit a new level. "Uncle Pat left some for me too?"

"That's right Vi. When she's old enough, though." Mum played with a strand of Violet's hair. "Since he didn't have any kids of his own, he wanted to make sure his nieces were taken care of." She sniffed. The memory of losing her brother was coming back to her. "I miss Pat, but knowing he is looking out for you two makes my heart melt. He loved you like his own."

"Mum." I reached across and hugged her. "Uncle Pat was the best, and I can't believe how generous he was. We miss him too." I pulled back. "But right now? I seriously need to take a selfie and post this online!"

Taking an emotional break while I snapped a picture of my new house keys, Mum opened a bottle of prosecco and handed the glasses around. Violet getting a glass of fizzy drink. When I had hashtagged the life out of my comments, I posted the picture and awaited messages from my besties, who would no doubt scream about house parties. All I was thinking about was how grateful I was to my late Uncle Pat and getting Owen over to celebrate!

"Shall we do another before we prepare the rest of dinner?" Dad winked at me. "Perhaps you'd like to give Violet her present, Ruby? Then we can do the rest later?"

"I would love to." Dad lent back in his favourite chair, watching us. "Vi?" I said, revealing the pretty lace gift bag I almost lost the night before. "Come sit with me." I tapped the space next to me.

Hopping over, I only just managed to get a pillow down before she landed on the hard floor.

"This is for you." I handed the bag to her. "It's not a new home, but I think, no, I know you'll love it."

Her eyes lit up in excitement. "What is it?"

"Open it and you'll find out."

Violet got to work, pulling the seal open of the lace bag which revealed the purple paper that the sales assistant of Selfridges expertly wrapped. Violet admired the paper that sparkled under the lights from the Christmas tree. It didn't take long for the white ribbon to be dismissed and to be turned into another Alice band. This time for her. We were like Alice in Wonderland and the Queen of Hearts auditionees. Ripping the paper, the box peaked through the purple. She looked up at me. She knew what was inside. A huge grin spread across her face.

"Is it?"

I nodded at the box. She took the hint and opened the lid to reveal the baby pink unicorn necklace. The colours matched her attire for the day.

"OMG!" She threw her arms around me, crushing me into an embrace. "How did you know, Ruby?"

"You have been dropping hints since the summer Vi."

"Thank you." She screamed. "Can I wear it now?"

"Of course you can." I took the necklace out of its velvet casing and placed it around her neck, fastening the clasp. "There."

Mum and Dad were almost in tears watching our exchange and were filming the moment on their phones.

This was one of those moments I wanted to remember forever. Even when Violet turns into a stroppy teenager, I will always be there for her and would do anything to make her happy. A bit like what Owen had done the previous night, but maybe I'll tell her the story of how I almost lost her Christmas present another day.

THE END

**Arguing whether
the answer is 8 or 10,
but your answer
was blue!
AmyC. Beckinsale**
©AmyCBeckinsale2022

CHAPTER ONE
Ben Garrison

Rewind to March 2020. Britain has just been put into lockdown for the first time and oh boy, we were not ready for it. Ok, so the world didn't expect the virus to spread so fast, but we did not expect the rules to be so strict. It made me realise how much we took for granted before the lockdown. Being able to go shopping, hug one another, eat out, snog someone!

That's when I decided to do what the entire world was doing. Virtual Quiz Nights! But not like any other quiz you'd expect. Oh, hell no! Not with our group of nutters! Nutters who mean the world to me.

My friends are like family and I miss my family, so all I'm going to say is thank the Lord for social media. Can you imagine having to live through, what will probably be taught in schools for years to come, history without seeing your BFF's faces? Yeah, me neither, which is why we are planning this evening, even if it is through a screen.

Just be warned, be very warned.

Love, Ben Xx

The First Quiz - 'Tame'

I poured myself another glass of wine as I waited for the attendees to join the virtual quiz my boyfriend, Martin and I were hosting. Eight o'clock. They should be arriving soon. A notification sounded from the speaker of my laptop. Emma, and her partner's face, Tom, filled my screen. I miss them. Another notification. Megan, my BFF, and her fiancé, Aidan. I waved frantically, loving how they were all waving back at me. My evening was almost complete, but as my laptop continued to sound, we were pleasantly surprised to find Owen and Clare joining at the same time Lucy and Kev arrived. It was a full house!

"Can you see me?" I asked, tilting the laptop screen higher to fit myself and my boyfriend Martin in. "Is that better?"

"Any lower Ben and we're gonna see more than your face," Emma, one of my many girlfriends from home, said. "Please tell me you have bottoms on this time?"

"It's ok Em. He's covered," Martin said, taking over the tilting of the screen.

I need to make a point here. Emma used to live in Somerset with us, along with Lucy and my best friend of all, Megan. The mischief we got up to? Well, that is for another time!

"How long is this gonna go on for Ben? Not that I'm nagging you along, it's just I've got Mum calling me in an hour."

"That, I can't guarantee Kev. I'll aim for an hour, but if you need to take the call, go ahead. It's not like Lucy will need you for the answers anyway," I teased, knowing full well that two of the participants would jump on the remark.

Queue the big leagues; Aidan and Owen in 3... 2... 1......

"You might need to wait a bit if you were baiting for a comment Ben," Megan said. "The guys are knackered from organising who's working from home at JMC and who's gonna keep coming in." She nudged Aidan's thigh.

No response? This is rare! These lads didn't get where they are today without the skill of quick wit. They ran one of the largest tech companies in the country. JMC Ltd. Specialising in computer software, apps, security, you name it, they did it! I literally handed them an easy kill on a silver platter. Nothing. They really must be as exhausted as Megan says. Even Kev, who worked for JMC, let the sly comment slide. This was weird!

"But you need not worry. I'm taking good care of him."

"You better be Meg, and you other ladies better be looking after you men too, I might add."

"What about them looking after us?" Clare asked.

"Oh please," Owen, her husband, said. "You can't seriously complain about the lifestyle you live?"

Clare shrugged. "Fair point."

One day, I will be a gentleman of leisure while my man brings the dollar in. Megan and Clare have it made.

The freedom to hit the shops, whenever they wished of the day, while Aidan and Owen ran the major tech company. One day Ben, one day!

"Ok, I would like to announce that the quiz is ready!" Martin said. Holding up his tablet. "Are we ready?"

A resounding 'Yeah' came from the group, and before Martin began with the first round, I took a moment to take a screenshot of the night before the games began. Five rectangles with five fabulous couples, and yes, I included myself and Martin in that compliment! For now? #LetTheGameBegin!

First round. History! Question One...

"In 1066, what battle took place in Britain?" Martin asked, watching notepads being lifted up so other contestants couldn't 'hear,' the answer. "Guys, you know the notepads don't work, right?, We can still hear you. Mute when discussing please?"

"Yes, sir!" Tom, Owen's brother and Emma's boyfriend said.

"Next question," Martin said, not giving the teams time to write their answers down!

"Hang on, HANG ON!" Lucy demanded, still scribbling frantically in her notebook.

"You have 5, 4, 3, 2, 1...Time up! Question two," I donned my best game show host voice. "Who led the Scottish army to victory over the English at the battle of Bannockburn in 1314?" Someone's phone sounded. "Whoever that is, turn it off, I'm not having any cheats on my quiz"

"Hang on mate, it's my mum, she's calling early," Kev said, answering the call. Poor Lucy had to think of the answer on her own. "Mum, hi, listen. Can I call you back?... Why, because I told you I have a video chat with our friends... Ugh, don't be like that..."

"Kevin, kitchen if you're gonna nag your Mother" Lucy pointed behind her, then faced the screen to find everyone pulling the same face. "Sorry guys, she's only worried about him being in the city."

"Naturally Lu," Megan said. "I don't blame her, I hate I can't get on a plane and check on Mum and Dad in the states, but at least we're lucky enough to have technology to get through this lockdown."

Kev rubbed his head. Believe me, I miss my parents as much as everyone else during this and what we are now calling 'living through history,' but Kev looked exhausted from the pressure.

"You alright, mate?" Tom asked him.

"Yeah, I'm good. She's not finding this lockdown easy. I'm here, my brother's up in Birmingham and apparently dad is driving her around the bend, so guess who's being used as a therapy tool?" He tapped his thighs. "What was the question again?"

After the first round was over, we ventured into the remaining subjects. My choice; Fashion. I knew from the second I announced the subject that Lucy (PA to the most prestigious fashion organisation in London) would get all the answers right, no matter how hard I made them. Ten rounds, comprising 10 questions each, and we were done.

Now? Now it was answer time and to find out who was to take the trophy of pride, and who was to host the next quiz... Drum roll, please!

*****

Ten thirty and the members of the quiz who were still working, even if it was from home, were starting to look tired. The idea of working from home does not appeal to me in the slightest. Here's a round of applause to them for having to drag their butts out of bed in the morning, only to stay at home and encourage themselves to get to work. As much as I'm missing my own work colleagues, in the shop I have been in for more than a decade, I know I couldn't do what they do. I need to be out, listening to music, meeting members of the public and encouraging their credit card out of their wallets! And I most certainly do not envy Martin. Trying to teach his class of IT students via zoom and keep their attention when they are clearly taking selfies and comments on each other's social posts from below the camera. Exactly what Owen Turner is doing right at this moment!

"Mr. Turner!" I shouted.

"What?" Tom Turner demanded, clearly thinking he must be doing something wrong with our realising he actually was!

"Not you Tom. Your brother!" Aidan chucked. Amused that Owen was about to get an ear slashing. "Get. Off. Your. Phone!"

Owen held his hands up in defence and threw the device out of shot. "I wasn't doing anything."

"Busted!" Clare said, leaning back on their deep purple velvet sofa. "I bloody warned you."

"The quiz is over though, right?"

"Nice try," Megan said. She knew the rules. She'd taken part in quizzes with me before. "The question round is over, however..." She wagged a finger at the screen. "We still need to find out the answers, so no trying to Google and change your answers at the last minute, Turner!"

"That's my girl," Aidan leaned across and kissed her head. "Never been so hot for you until right now."

"Fuck's sake Aid!" Owen rolled his eyes. He held his hands up. "Look, no phone, happy?"

"Clare?" Emma asked.

"Nah, he's good. In fact," She stole the notepad from him. "I will check the answers off."

Martin was sitting crossed legged, waiting patiently like he did when his students weren't paying attention. It was hilarious how he was treating our closest friends like a group of teenagers. He coughed, quickly getting everyone's attention.

"Oh, oh I'm sorry. Are we all finished now?" He raised one eyebrow. "Then I shall begin. Mark your points by each round then text us your results and we'll announce who sucks to who's the smart ass."

We flew through the answers, only stopping to debate when someone was determined that they were right and we must have made up the answer. As I predicted, Lucy had gotten all the fashion questions right. It was obvious, she literally fist bumped the air every time Martin released the answer.

"I am sooooo gonna win, bitches!"

"Hey!" Kev objected. "I helped."

"Hardly babe, you thought the answer to 'what does EA stand for' meant 'Ever After.'" She ruffled his hair. "There isn't even a designer called that. Emporio Armani, dumbass!"

Round after round, the answers were given, and after each round four texts came through. So far, Emma and Tom were winning, but after the final round, anything could happen. General Knowledge.

"No! NO!" Aidan demanded. "That can't be the answer. You have to be fucking kidding me."

Warning. The CEO of the group loves to drop the odd one or two swear words when he doesn't get his way!

"Sorry, Aidan, but Google doesn't lie. Joe Biden's middle name is not Robert," Martin assured him. "Zero points."

"Send me your last texts guys." I said, already adding up the previous rounds. The texts came in and we had our results. "Are you ready?"

"Ready to go to bed?" Emma said sarcastically as Tom leaned his head on her shoulder, already looking like he'd passed out.

"In last place, and sure to sulk for the rest of the lockdown... Aidan and Megan!" Aidan threw the paper in the air, making a mess all around them. "In third? Lucy and Kev!" They clapped, politely. "And in second place," I drum rolled on my knee, since everyone would know who the winners were about to be. "Emma and Tom, which means this week's winners are Clare and Owen!"

They literally jumped in, celebrating the win, but Tom had words to share.

"How do we know he wasn't cheating the whole time? We all saw the phone?"

"Ahh, Tom, little bro. Don't be such a sore loser. The only person who needs to be getting the stick is Aid!"

"Fuck off!" Aidan spat out, now sat back down on the white sofa as Megan stroked his hair in comfort, trying not to laugh at his childlike state.

Owen reached behind himself and pulled out a silver clipboard. "I hope you're ready for next week guys, because we came prepared."

"Dear Lord," Aidan rolled his eyes. "He's already got something planned. Shot me now."

"Dear sweet Aidan, don't be a diva. You'll like this game," He tapped the clipboard. "I know for sure, this one is right up your street."

CHAPTER TWO
Owen Turner

Last week, my wife and I won the quiz, much to my brother and best mate's disapproval. Aidan was not happy, and it was hilarious. I've worked with the guy every day, for the past sixteen years. He was the best man at our wedding. We run a company together and as much as he makes life a handful sometimes, I love the guy. Yeah, I love a guy. Quick, head to the tabloids! 'Owen Turner admits his love for Aidan Costello'. Fuck the lot of you, he's like a brother to me. Dammit, I'm getting off topic.

What's annoying about this lockdown? I suppose not being able to see my actual brother, Tom and our family. Having to work from home and not be in the office. Do you know what else I miss? McDonalds, Burger King, that barbecue place we visit at least once a month near Tower Bridge. Fast food, good food, grilled food and a nice ice-cold beer from a frosted glass. Excuse me while I drool on my lap. My wife would murder me if she found out how much junk food we eat at work. Can we make this out secret? One to keep between you and me? Great, thanks. On that note, best sign into the meeting and see what crazy things the guys have been up to this week!

Owen Turner, vice CEO of JMC Ltd

The Second Quiz - 'Game Time'

"Is he going to be long Meg?" I asked, waiting for Aidan to be done on the phone. He'd been talking for the good part of an hour, and I knew he was checking in on Nick.

"Sounds like they're finishing up now Owen." Megan turned in her seat to find Aidan rubbing his forehead before running his hand through his hair and hanging up.

I should keep you updated. Nick is a doctor at Farnham hospital where he and his wife, Lydia, live with their daughter, Sara. He's a magnificent doctor and has treated more than a few of us over the years. He's also

Aidan's oldest friend, so there is no doubt Aid's worried about him and his family during this historic moment in time.

History 101; The Pandemic of 2020.

Aidan sat on his sofa, running a hand over his eyes again. "Sorry guys."

"How's Nick?" Kev asked, taking a sip of diet coke.

"Knackered." Aidan said, leaning forward. "He's been doing thirty-six-hour shifts." There was an intake of breath from everyone in the group chat. "He's not getting much of a break in between before he has to do it again. Lyd's naturally worried he'll burn out, but he's not gonna stop. Said the entire NHS is all hands on."

"Christ," I ran my own hand across my eyes. "Makes you respect the health service more, right?"

"They are literally the saviours of the country." Emma said.

"We should do something," Clare said, clapping her hands together in excitement. "Well, JMC should."

"Like what?" I ask, sensing a crazy idea forming in my wife's mind.

"Raise some funds for them by doing something ridiculous, something the public can get behind and get involved with, too. Like…" Here we go, here comes the idea of making everyone at JMC, especially me and Aid, squirm. "… virtual online dates for a cost?"

"I'd rather just give them a million quid than do that Clare." Aidan had his head back in his hands again. He must be finding it hard not to check in on Nick.

Lucy coughed, trying to break the focus. "Guys, what are we doing this evening?"

I swear, it was clear to all of us. Aidan lifting his head and mouthing 'thank you' to Lucy. I composed myself and set out the rules, and explained what was going to happen by pulling out the silver clipboard.

"I hope you are all feeling at the top of your game tonight guys, because this is going to get physical!"

*****

"Come on, Emma!" Tom screamed. "Come on! You can do it. No, not in the kitchen. The hallway, THE

HALLWAY!"

Emma came running back into the living room, completely out of breath and panting like she'd run a marathon. She held up an umbrella to the screen.

"I. Am. NOT. Doing. That. Again." She insisted.

I checked the time on the tablet that was counting down the seconds she had to find the object which was requested. "Hmmm, Em, you missed it by four seconds. No points."

We all had to laugh when her face turned from triumph to full pout and a look of hatred for me.

"I hate the Turner brothers sometimes, you know." She slumped back on the sofa, dismissing the umbrella, and tried her best to hide a snigger trying to escape.

The game? Have you got it yet? Yeah, we have our closet pals running around their houses searching for objects. Each object they find within the time allocated, thirty seconds, then they are awarded points. Ben and Martin are winning right now, mainly because they share a two-bedroom flat so they don't have to run around too far, unlike Aidan and Megan. They chose to leave London when the lockdown was due to be announced and are in their large luxurious barn conversion in Farnham. Yeah, that's another Aid's been bummed out. He's only a few miles from Nick and Lydia and can't see them. I swear if they come last again, Aidan is gonna be more deadly than the virus sweeping the world!

"Alright, who's next," Clare leans across to me, and checks the list. "Lucy and Kev! Who's gonna take this one, guys?"

"Yo!" Kev shoots his hand up.

"Alright Kev," I said. "You have thirty seconds to produce and make a cocktail," Kev readies himself, sitting on the edge of the sofa. "Ready and GO!"

Lucy followed him with what I could only assume was a tablet, into the kitchen he was already throwing spirits together. His speed was something else, and it was nice to see that his knowledge as a bartender hadn't been forgotten. We met Kev the same night Aidan fell in love with Megan at a club in Leicester Square and well, one thing led to another and we kinda adopted him!

"Come on, Kevin!" Lucy screamed as everyone joined

in, egging him on. "Come on!"

"There!" He placed the 'made up on the spot' cocktail on the kitchen island, spilling a bit. He picked up a tea towel and wiped around the surface, just like the trained bartender he still is. "Stop that clock Turner!" He knew he had time to spare.

"Lucy?" I ask. "Would you do the honours?"

She picked up the cocktail, taking a sniff to try to work out its ingredients. Happy, she took a sip and mulled it over before posting her lips and nodding. "A hint of vanilla, followed by a liquor that burns the back of your throat!" She coughed lightly, then took another sip. "Still, it's good."

Kev threw his hands in the air. "Add the points up, Mr. Turner, that is a total win!"

Megan was massaging Aidan's shoulders as he readied himself to run around their barn to find one of our company's original designs he'd drawn up when he was at University. He knew exactly where it was, but like I said, that barn is massive! He was even wearing his running trainers to grip the floor better.

"GO!" I shouted, only for him to remain sitting on the sofa. Instead, he flipped his phone open, and produced a group of files named, 'Software Idea - No1'. They had completely played us all! He turned the phone around and there it was, clear as day. The concept idea for one of JMC's flagship programmes. Shit! I stopped the clock, which had only counted down from thirty to twenty. Maximum points. He dropped his phone in a 'mic drop' style, looking smug as Megan flipped us all off looking as full of it as her pig-headed prick of a man was!

"Arseholes!" my brother said, looking like he was about to have a strop.

"Come up and join the big leagues Tom," Aidan replied, relaxing and taking a long sip of his beer. He lifted his hand, which Megan quickly responded with by giving him a high-five. "Someday, you might catch up with us."

I tallied up the scores. It was looking close. One more challenge and we would know the winner.

"Right, this is the last challenge guys and involves the woman," I said. "But there is a twist."

"Hang on," Martin held his hand up, like he was in a classroom. He pointed between himself and Ben. "Someone needs to decide."

"Ben!" Everyone answered the obvious question who the woman in their relationship was. Ben didn't even argue. He just readied himself to hear the instructions.

"As I was saying. The twist. As this is the final round, you are all going to do the task," I paused for dramatic effect. "together!"

A resounding, 'ohhh' came across the zoom call.

"I truly hate you right now," Tom complained. "As of now, I have no brother."

"But you look adorable!" Emma said, pinching his cheeks. Each gentleman on the screen is giving me dagger eyes, underneath a fresh coat of makeup. When I set the counter and shouted for the ladies to get to work, they all reached for their cosmetic bags and began painting their men's faces with all colours of the rainbow and I know what you're going to ask me. Ben had a cosmetic bag, full of makeup? Yeah, he did, and I don't want to know why! Admiring the four rectangles in front of me, I take in each painted face. Tom is looking less than impressed, sporting a typical blue eyeshadow and red lip combo. Somehow, Megan found the time to apply kitten flick eyeliner on Aidan and matched the noir style with a clear sequin lip gloss. Probably something to do with her skills of being an artist. I hate to say it, but Aidan's actually pulling it off. Kev? Well, for a fashion expert with a mountain of style knowledge, Lucy had royally failed. He was sporting an orange face with a hint of mascara. He seriously looked like he'd stepped off the set for orange county, minus the county. Martin. Ok, how in the hell did Ben manage to pull off such a sophisticated look on him? This guy has skills! Clare judged the looks as I subtly took a screenshot of the little darlings as they gave me death glares. That was going straight onto my social pages as soon as I hung from the call.

"Yep, yeah." Clare said, tapping at the calculator on her phone and I read out the previous scores before we announced the makeover winner. I looked up at the screen to catch Aidan and Megan taking a selfie on his phone. He was pouting! That was going to be only before I even posted mine. "Ok guys, we have just added up the previous scores and in the lead before this 'stunning' round, was Lucy and Kev."

"Fuck yeah!" Kev yelled, fist bumping Lucy.

"But all could change. We have the final scores of this task. Each team will be given several points as per their position, so with no more delay in fourth place is," I paused for dramatic effect. "Kev and Lucy, scoring a shameful five points for that orange monstrosity."

"I ran out of time!" Lucy protested. "Ten more seconds and I would have had it."

"No, you wouldn't have Lucy." Emma teased.

Clare took over. "In third and getting ten points for the dated look, Tom and Emma!"

Tom turned to Emma. "Does this mean I can take this crap off now?"

Emma pulled her phone out and opened the camera. She took a shot of his made-up face. "Now you can."

"From what Clare says, this took some deciding, but the winner of the round and getting twenty points, leaving the runner-up to receive fifteen is Megan," She literally jumped off the sofa, pulling Aidan into a hug. "For getting that eyeliner so perfect. It looks like a professional makeup artist did it!"

"Bloody fix," Ben protested, throwing a makeup brush on the floor. "She's an artist. She literally has the qualification to say so."

Aidan leaned in, fluttering his eyes. "Don't be such a hard loser Benjamin." He blew him a kiss, which soon quietened him down.

"Who's the overall winner Owen?"

I tally up the totals. The lead took an impressive jump forward from that final round.

"Get ready for the ego to go into full overdrive guys, because this week's winners are..."

CHAPTER THREE
(Two Weeks Later)
Aidan Costello

First things first. Whatever Owen told you about me is
not true. Well, some of it is. I was the best man at his
wedding, I have worked with him for longer than I
probably should have and he is like the brother I never
had as well and yes, he's a twat for making us sit and let
the girls put makeup on us. Believe me, when I say that
payback has been mentally stored for future use and I'm
sorry to the guys that they've had to wait a few weeks
for the next game night. We had priorities that needed to
be taken care of. Perks of being the boss of a major tech
company during a pandemic!

   Is this where I tell you about myself? Yeah? Surely
you know the basics from the media? No? Where have
you been? Fine, I'll tell you, a bit. CEO of JMC, my own
company based in the city. Engaged to the most
amazing, beautiful and strong woman I have ever met;
Megan Ashton. She's been my savour, but that's a whole
different story. Orphaned at six when my parents were
killed in a car crash in Ireland. Made it my absolute
mission to take over the world and make a name for
myself, in my parents' memory. And that's all you're
getting. Want more? Google it.

   Aidan Costello ;)

The Third Quiz - 'What Quiz?'

Kev - Anyone heard anything from them?
Emma - Megan said that Aidan was on another work call,
@OwenTurner, you on that call as well?
Owen - Nope, feeling rejected right now
Emma - Sorry Kev, Owen knows nothing
Kev - In the same group chat Em!
Megan - Shit is going down...!
Owen - Fan-fucking-tasitic
Clare - @OwenTurner LANGUAGE!
Tom - Listen to the wife bro, or your arse is toast!
Clare - It's always toasted @TomTurner

Lucy - Have I got time to wash my hair? I feel gross
Kev - You're not gross babe, you're always stunning to me.
Tom - Excuse me while I throw up!
Emma - Hey, has @BenGarrison or @MartinRoberts checked in yet?
Ben - We're here, just waiting for you guys to stop bickering
Megan - #GoodCall
Owen - Hashtags? Really? Are we teenagers again?
Megan - You wanna tell JMC's social media team that?
Owen - No
Aidan - Sorry guys. @OwenTurner, remind me to update you later
Owen - What's up @AidanCostello
Aidan - Some of the staff working in Canary have the virus. Need to reevaluate the 'work from home' procedure and organise a deep clean
Owen - Gotcha boss

This royally sucks! I feel so fucking unless sat at home and not be able to drop everything to help and support my JMC family through what I can only imagine to be hell on earth. I'd seen the news, we all had. I've always been there for anyone in that office if they need me, and this is killing me. At least they all have mine and Owen's direct numbers, work and personal if they need to talk, but for me? Yeah, that's not nearly enough. We've all watched The Walking Dead, surely we can 'Rick Grimes' it up and beat our way into the city to help? Yeah, I know. Don't be such an idiot Costello. The police wouldn't give a fuck who I am, they'd just slap a fine on my lap and give me an almighty bollocking. Even for trying to do the right thing. Ok, why are we here? Oh right, this bloody game we seemed to have turned into a tradition.

"Aid," Megan said, rubbing my arm. "You ok?"

"Yeah, sorry baby," I rubbed my eyes, trying desperately to regain my focus. "Mind's elsewhere."

"You need to let us help take the weight off. You're being too hard on yourself again."

How is she reading my mind?

"Meg is right, dude," Owen said over the stereo system. I linked up to the flatscreen displayed on the wall ahead of us. I didn't even notice Megan opening the video chat. All four windows looked back at me in concern. "Take this opportunity to try to relax. It's the only real thing we can do at this point in time."

"Really Owen? Really?"

"It is getting harder, isn't it?" Lucy said, looking directly at the floor.

Oh, god, I've bummed everyone out. They're all sitting there looking back at me like Iron Man has died for the second time. I've got to turn this call around. Somehow.

"Listen, guys," I clapped my hands together. One of my trademark 'Aidan is fine, move on' moves. "Let's get on with why we're all here."

"Are you sure you don't want to give it a miss this week?" Lucy asked. "You know, if you have a lot on your mind?"

She's sweet, but no. I need a distraction. Instead of giving my reasons why I don't need another week off, even though I could happily give it a miss and spend the evening with Megan in the pool, I just get on with the game.

"Since we've done a quiz and had a workout last week, we thought we'd play something different."

"Which is?" Ben asked.

"Charades." Megan replied, holding her hands above her head and drawing a rainbow. "We'll be placed into groups and take it in turn to act out the film, movie, book or television show Aidan texts."

"Sounds like the standard rules of charades, so far, but go on." Owen said, knowing full well there was going to be something different to this game.

"We've decided your teams," Megan said. "Listen closely, as I will announce them only once."

*****

This is going to scar me for life! The vision of Kev gyrating against the arm of the sofa will haunt me for years.

Every face on the call was in shock, laughing, or covering their eyes in shame at the dance moves Kev was pulling. He was trying his best to make it as obvious to Clare as he could. Unfortunately the gyrating wasn't helping.

"Can you give me a clue that will actually help?" Clare begged. "Anything to stop you from putting us all in therapy."

Kev flung his hands in the air, then snapped his fingers.

What in the hell is he doing now? I mean, I know what he's trying to do, I text him the challenge, but this? This is a mixture of blackmail for years to come and humiliation, especially when he finds out we've recorded the entire thing.

Kev was prancing around the living room of the house he shares with Lucy, slapping his own arse.

"OH! OH!" Clare pointed at the screen. "Horse racing? Umm, is it Frankie Dettori?"

Kev rolled his eyes and began humping the sofa again. "It's so obvious!"

"It so isn't!" Clare snapped.

"Horses and dancing?" Martin said. They were all trying to guess now. "I just can't see where the connection is."

"You're getting somewhere with the horse reference Clare," I said, wanting to get this torture over with. "But think more 'pony'."

Megan's eyes lit up. I'm pretty sure she's got it and pretty sure, no, absolutely sure she's seen the movie this actor is connected to. Probably the sequel too!

"Pony? How is that meant to help Aidan?"

Clare was rounding onto me now. Her temper was hilarious to witness and over the years I had been on the other end of it more times than I'd like to say. Mainly when Owen's come home trashed after a night out!

"Wait just a minute." She whispered into Owen's ear. His face scrunched up. He was visualising it, and most likely Kev was in the lead role!

"Bloody hell," He faced the screen. "Is it Channing Tatum?"

"YES!" Kev applauded him.

"And those iconic dance moves," Ben waved a hand. "were meant to be his very fine, and sexy dance in Magic Mike?" Kev nodded. Ben got closer to the screen. "Don't give up the day job Kevin."

I marked a point for Clare, things were looking close and now it was Tom's turn. If someone would be happy to make a complete dick out of themselves, it was Thomas Turner! Brace yourselves. You thought Kev's performance was bad?

"Ok Tom, it's your turn to try to convince Ben." I sent the message, angling my phone screen to Megan. I couldn't resist.

"Aidan," Tom said, staring me down after reading the text. "You're a twat!"

As the game continued into the evening, after Ben had guessed in record time that Tom was acting out 'The Little Mermaid', a secret favourite film from his childhood, I couldn't help but notice my work phone lighting up every five seconds with notifications from my staff. What in the hell is going on now? How many more people were feeling unwell? Physically and mentally. I had to end this game. I needed to check on them. Luckily, my goddess fiancée noticed too and took charge of the game. I gave Owen a look only he would get and quickly slipped out of view. Missed calls, texts, voicemails, emails. This was getting out of hand. As much as I hated to admit it, I had to take on Lucy's suggestion. I needed a break. Here goes nothing.

"You ok babe?" Megan asked me, already sensing the answer that was coming.

"I'm good," I addressed the smiling faces looking back at me as I sat back down. "Guys, we need to make this the last round."

Owen's smile faded. "More?" I nodded. "Shit," He rubbed his temples. "Aid, add up the totals, we'll finish now, if that's ok with everyone. Aidan and I have work to do."

A resounding response came through the speakers of my laptop, all agreeing that it was time to stop. God, I love these guys. There isn't a single thing I wouldn't do for them.

"I appreciate it. Thank you. Owen?"

"Yeah mate."

"I'll set up another call shortly. Let me check these messages, then we can hit it head on."

"You got it Aid."

Everyone hung up, agreeing to meet up again for a virtual game when the time was right.

"Aidan?" Megan said. Her voice sounded full of concern. I already knew where this was going. "What can I do to help?"

CHAPTER FOUR
(One Month Later)
Megan Ashton

Here we are, together in spirit, but physically apart. We haven't done a quiz for a few weeks now, and I'm missing the banter. It's not like we've not spoken to our friends and family, of course we have. The occasional phone call and video chat, but nothing beats being able to sit in a beer garden and talk. Face to face. This is hard, like really hard.

Last Thursday, we took part in clapping for our country's National Health Service. Everyone in the UK stood out on their doorsteps and applauded their hard work. One nation coming together to recognise our heroes.

Every night, Aidan and I watch the updates from the government, hoping for some kind of miracle or hope. This is going to be a long waiting game, I can tell but as long as we all do as we're told, we will come out the other end of this. I can't wait to see my friends.

Aidan and Owen have been working their butts off to try to support their employees as much as they can. JMC is like an extension of family in their eyes and I know they will do absolutely anything to be there for them. And time of day or night.   Since this isn't leading up to another quiz, I should tell you, I'm not sitting here talking to myself. No, I've not gone lockdown stir crazy, just yet. I began writing a daily diary. I mean, what else am I going to do? I can't exactly nip into London and hit Oxford Street. Visit Carnaby Street and buy more shoes. The shops are shut. I would bake a batch of cakes, but as well as the loo roll shortage (people going crazy over Andrex), self-rising flour seems to fly off the shelves, too. #BananaBread! SIGH! There is always another movie marathon, hit the home gym, get around to cleaning the fridge freezer like we keep saying we're going to do.

    "MEGAN!!!"

Is it me? Or does that sound like Aidan needs me?

Testing Times - "No Quiz"

Here is what I've learnt about my fiancé since we've been together. When he shouts like that through the house, either something is wrong, or he's lost something. He's had a software breakthrough and absolutely has to tell me straight away, even though I will have no idea what he's on about, or there's been a news update. My guess is that he's abandoned his work and is sitting on the sofa, feet up, cuddling a fresh black coffee with a muffin in the other, watching the tv.

"What is it babe?" Oh look, I won, he's exactly where I said he'd be.

"There's an update," He tapped the sofa, summoning me like a puppy. "Sit,"

I scoot in next to him, placing my feet next to his on the coffee table. The Prime Minister was addressing the nation. We sat in silence, fingers crossed, watching and listening intently. I couldn't quite believe my ears; we could go out. Not 'out, out', but we could sit in parks. Oh, happy days! I love this barn conversion, but to see a different part of the town? I felt like a five-year-old girl at Christmas!

"I know you're excited, sweetheart, and believe me, I am too, but we still need to be cautious."

"I know, but sitting in the park never seems so damn exciting until now!"

The group chat started going bat shit crazy. They all must have been watching.

Ben - We're not grounded anymore!

Emma - Seriously, can't tell you how sick I am of these walls

Tom - Is that directed at me @EmmaRowe?

Emma - Don't be such a princess. Of course not @TomTurner

Clare - Are we allowed to meet up yet then?

Kev - Didn't sound like it @ClareTurner

Lucy - He said we can sunbathe, so if we're spaced out, that should be ok?

Martin - Yeah, you and everyone else in London

Lydia - @MartinRobinson makes a good point. Everyone will be out!

Megan - Am I the only one who heard him say they might start thinking about opening shops?

Aidan - Of course you heard that @MeganAshton ;)

Owen - Gonna spend all of @AidanCostello's cash @MeganAshton

Megan - Not all of it

Aidan - Don't encourage it @OwenTurner!

"So, we could sunbathe. Sit in the park. That's great and all, but we still can't see friends?" I asked. "Is that right?"

"I don't know. Lucy has a point, and so does Martin. Will everyone take a mile when only an inch has been given?"

"Only one way to find out?" Aidan said. "Wait a week and watch the news reports."

I rolled my head back, landing on the back of the sofa. "So, we're still grounded?"

*****

Oh boy, was Aidan right! As soon as the rules were lifted, it went insane. Parks were flooded with people wanting to enjoy the outdoors and the glorious weather we were having. It was like a festival on the coast and we all knew what that would mean? As much as I hated not being about to go about my daily life, I knew I had to stay put. I opened the group chat.

Megan - So, who wants to take on the helm of being the next quiz master?
...

I knew from the lack of responses no one wanted to wage in on that conversation. Nothing else to do than re-watch the entire series of 'Friends'.

Sat in bed, in my pyjamas, under the covers. I destroyed a pot of Ben & Jerry's Cookie Dough ice cream as Joey announced that doesn't share food. Exactly what I was doing right now, when Aidan joined me. Landing face down on his pillow in a grump.

"That good of a day, was it?"

He lifted his head so I could hear him. "I'm thinking JMC isn't worth it."

"What?" I abandoned the ice cream, not that there was much left. This was much more important than the delicious, creamy, smooth...Dammit, focus! "What brought this on?"

"There are hundreds of tech companies, what's the point in having another one?"

Ok, so we're bummed out for not being in the office and getting a kick out of creating new software programmes and spending time with the 'work' family.

"And you'd be happy to throw it all away, give up, let down an entire workforce and make them unemployed, would you?"

"No," He mumbled into the pillow. "Just can't be arsed anymore."

Great, a stubborn CEO having a strop! I let out a long sigh and grabbed my phone. "Hey, call Owen Turner." It didn't take long for Owen to answer the video call, his non shaved face filled my screen. He seriously needed a haircut!

"Hey Meg. How's things? You and Aidan, ok?"

"Oh, you know, same stuff, different day."

"What's wrong Meg?" He asked, cottoning Aidan's position and already knowing why I called him.

I pointed at the ball of misery laying next to me. "This doughnut right here is thinking about giving up on JMC because he can't be arsed anymore," I gestured to his entire body. "Care to do what you do best?"

Owen pushed the sleeves up on his long sleeve top. I could literally sense the vibes coming from Aidan, knowing he was about to get a bollocking!

"Aidan James Costello," Oh, here we go. "Abandoning everything you have accomplished is simply not acceptable, you hear me?" Aidan turned over onto his back, leaning his head on my lap. He was listening and not even trying to argue. "I know what you're like when you're bummed out, and right now? Right now, you are doing a fine job of acting like a prat!"

(A few more weeks later)

Megan Ashton

The lockdown of 2020 is getting tougher. I love our home, but I would do anything to be back in the city. Don't get me wrong, there are perks. A beautiful barn conversion and a hot as hell finance to enjoy, all, to, myself? Thank you, universe!

We walked into town last week. Needed to pick up some basics from the supermarket. Yay! The weather was glorious! Claiming a park bench with our shopping bags and travel mugs from home, filled with Jack Daniels, we sat and watched the world go by. No one suspected we were day drinking in the local park. As far as anyone knew, we were drinking tea! The fact that our measures were larger than the average pub measure was no one else's business, expect us.

I had to wonder how the rest of the gang were up too. I opened our group chat and took a shot of Aidan and I chilled on the bench and sent it. Moments later, we'd received selfies from the entire group.

Ben - Looking good! Check out Mr Smooth, @AidanCostello in his sunglasses #Lush!
Aidan - Thanks, you're not having them
Ben - Dammit!
Owen - Have you two turned into an old couple already? Please tell me you're feeding ducks with leftover bread! LOL! :-0
Tom - And with their coco in travel mugs @OwenTurner!!
Megan - Far from it kids.
Clare - Did you guys hear? They are making another announcement this evening. #FingersCrossed!

"We should get back," Aidan said, getting to his feet and dragging me up with him. I will admit, I stumbled twice. "See what sort of hell on earth will be told today?"

CHAPTER FIVE
(A Couple of Days Later)
Tom Turner

I believe we haven't had the pleasure of meeting yet.
Name's Tom Turner. Brother of Owen, brother-in-law to
Clare. You get the gist. It has been a bitch for a couple
of months. Felt like years, if I'm honest. But today is the
day! The day we've been waiting for. The sun is out and
if Emma, my girlfriend, would hurry, we might enjoy it
before the sun sets.

Em and I both work in office jobs. Me? I'm an
architect and Em works at JMC, alongside Aidan, Owen
and Kev. We've been working from home throughout the
duration of the lockdown and so far we haven't managed
to piss each other off. Worked rather well, actually. We
set up a joint office, converting one of the spare rooms.
Half the room was Em's, the other mine. Mine being
closer to the window. Mainly so I could use the natural
light to draw up building plans. I could seriously see
myself working from home more often. Workload, sexy
girlfriend, fridge and food within reach whenever I
desired it.

But today? Today was going to be special..

We're Here, Where Are you?
"Can I be the first to tell you how much I've missed
your faces?" Kev said, sat on the grass with Lucy. "It's
been so hard."

"Christ, Kev's gonna start crying," Owen said.
"Someone chuck him a pack of Kleenex."

That's right. We're together at last!

"Why here? Emma asked, looking out over the skyline
of London.

"Apart from it being a great view?" Aidan said. "It's
peaceful? We can spread out and adhere to the distance
rules and, well, it's special."

"How?" Emma asked again.

"It's the first place Aidan took me the night we got
together. He wanted to show me how beautiful the city

could be at night."

"Yeah, right," Owen said, rolling his eyes. "Corny move Aid."

Aidan didn't bother arguing back, which was weird because those two always bicker at each other. It's part of what makes their friendship special!

We all saw the PM's report a few days ago and the updates which we were shitting ourselves about. If I'm honest, I thought the restrictions were going to get tougher and not the announcement that six people could meet up in an open location. Can you imagine how crazy our group chat went? I mean, you heard from Megan about what happened when they said we could sit in a park. That was NOTHING compared to this. Aidan and Megan were in the car and heading back to London to stay at their penthouse apartment on Southbank the next day. Owen was organising and planning a day in particular we could meet, making sure it wasn't going to disturb us meeting up with family and I was organising and seeing what we could do when we arrived at Parliament Hill in Hampstead Heath. Were we allowed to kick a ball around? Frisbee? In the end, we didn't need it. Kev was right, it was emotional to see each other in the flesh again. Please, please do not tell my brother I said that. I will never live it down. Ok, sure. We are no way near getting out of this pandemic, and we have a long way to go, but to see your friends, and family makes you realise how blessed you are. I love these guys, and hell, I might even ask Emma to marry me. Actually, you know what, I'm gonna do it. Afterall,l we had been through, I can't imagine my life without her now.

"How did Ben and Martin handle the announcement, Megan?" Clare asked.

Megan abandoned her attempt at opening a jar of jam, passing it to Aidan, who did the deed in one move. "They were as excited as we were Clare, although they wished they could be here with us."

"They are," Emma said. "In spirit."

As Ben and Martin were in a different part of the south of England, it wasn't possible for them to make the long journey to London yet. At least they could meet up with friends where they were.

"Did anyone bring any mayonnaise?" Lucy asked, wanting to add seasoning to her salad that she prepared.

Aidan threw a bottle across to her. "Go nuts."

"Thanks." She emptied most of the bottle on her tuna.

"Do you want some tuna with that?" Kev asked, watching her drown the food.

Megan, laid out on her and Aidan's blanket in shorts and a tank top enjoying the sun, waved in her direction. "She's always done that Kev, don't bother trying to change her."

"Thank you, Miss Ashton." Lucy gratefully said.

"You're welcome, Miss Stone."

Clare stood up and opened their ice cooler. "I don't know if anyone else thought about this, but we have some cold drinks." She produced some bottles of wine and beer. "Another good reason to pick this location. We can't be caught!"

"You are a genius Clare!" Emma said, picking up a glass and stretching as far as she could so Clare could pour her a glass of wine.

Sitting in silence as we enjoyed good food, drinks and amazing company, we stared out at the view ahead of us. London in all its glory, looked back at us like it was watching us, letting us know everything was going to be ok. That we still had one another and that we were going to come through it together.

I nudged Emma's side. She looked at me. She had so much love in her eyes. She was the only one for me. This was it. This was my moment.

"Marry me?"

THE END

Stand By Me
AmyC. Beckinsale

"Stand by lighting, stand by sound. Are the actors ready? Are my crew ready? No? Why not?"

Connor, the stage manager all the directors wanted, was in demand, but this show was going to push his temper and make him realise what was important in life. His career or his family?

CHAPTER ONE

I swear to all that is holy, if I hear another vase smash, I am going to hunt down that actor and summon the depths of hell in an almighty stage manager hissy fit! I've worked in theatre for almost ten years, professionally that is, and not once have I wanted to backhand an actor more! And that actor needs to be taken down a peg or two, maybe even three, plus.

I'm sure I'm not the only stage manager who's witnessed it, when the actors get given the boot to make way for that one performer who *always* gets cast in the leading role? And that performer who thinks they are above everyone else, including breaking the props that my assistant stage manager had searched high and low for, just so they can deliver their line while holding a vase of flowers to place on the makeshift window sill. How hard is it to walk stage right to the window and simply put the vase down? Easy as pie, right? Yeah, think again. For Kirina Jakson-Miles, it was a task she really felt was below her. Ladies and gents, I give you the diva. Kirina had been getting the lead roles the past few years, and between you and me, I was getting sick of it. The woman can act, she's extremely talented, it's the attitude that annoys me. All knowing, I'm the leading actress and you'll do as I say attitude. The attitude that makes her think she can treat my backstage crew like dirt. That we're not the ones who make her look good on stage. What I'd give to bring her down to earth.

"Connor?"

That's the voice of someone who's ready to have a fit. Time to go to work.

"Over here Heather."

My assistant stage manager, Heather, stormed up to me and lent on my makeshift bench in the auditorium. We were a week away from opening night, so my place was in front of the stage where I could see what was going down on the stage before they banished me to the blacks of the backstage area.

"What's up?"

"Kirina is up, that's what."

"Props?"

"I can't go into the store and buy another vase again Connor, it's embarrassing. The assistant is sure I have a fetish for long-stemmed vases." She hid her head in her hands. "God knows what he thinks I'm using them for." I tapped her head. "I'll go over after we've run this next scene."

"Thank you-"

"Talking props! Places. From the top of scene eight. We will run it until it is pristine."

We both sat up that little straighter at the sound of the director's voice booming through the theatre. Now it was time for the actors to get to work. Heather winked at me before taking her place backstage, leaving me to open my notes to scene eight and don my headset.

"Lighting and sound, are you there?"

"Loud and clear boss"

"Ok, here we go. SFX thirteen and LX eleven, standby..."

*****

Our director, Sean, wasn't joking when he said he wanted to run the scene until it was pristine. We must have had to stop at least three times per run. Even Kirina was getting tired and she had only been at the theatre since midday. The crew were there at the crack of dawn. I say the crack of dawn. That's probably being dramatic, but it was certainly earlier than the cast. My wife, Monica was sending me texts asking when I was to be expected home earlier, but she gave up when it hit ten o'clock. By the time I get on the tube and walk through the door, she'd be fast asleep. Not that I blame her. If I was in her position, I would do the same.

Monica and I met when I was a runner for a show of the west end. She and her Mum were having a ladies night out and I happened to be coming out from the backstage area after the show with a handful of wigs that needed special attention. Special attention meaning they needed to be washed and tidied up before the following night's show. She sniggerd at me, trying to control the mess in my arms and I found myself laughing with her. We just clicked, you know. It was like I knew that one day I was going to marry this woman one day and I did. Six years after we met I'd tracked her down, asked her out on a date and now we were husband and wife with a beautiful baby girl, Katie-May.

"Connor!"

I spun around just seconds before I escaped the theatre.

"Sean?"

What does he want now?

"Got a minute?"

Not really.

"Sure. What's up?"

He placed an arm around my shoulders. The way someone does when they are about to ask you for a favour. And when Sean did the manoeuvre, it meant he wanted something.

"I know I said you could have the morning off tomorrow, but I need you."

"Come on Sean. You know I need the morning to take Katie-May for her shots. Monica's working and he can't find anyone to cover her shifts."

Sean groaned and rubbed his temples with his thumb and forefinger. "It's just this scene. It doesn't feel right yet. We need to run it again."

I rounded on him. This guy needs to learn to accept that if the actors aren't going to pull something spectacular out of their arses, then it's too late. That or he's cast the wrong people all together.

"For the love of Christ, Sean. We ran it how many times tonight? The actors were tired. You pushed them so much, what else do you expect? They need rest. You need to let them recharge and psyche themselves up for opening night. Not run one scene repeatedly because you're not happy. And I need tomorrow morning off to take my daughter to the doctors. End of discussion."

Sean folded his arms and raised one eyebrow. Like that was going to scare me. This guy was a pansy compared to some directors I've worked with.

"So, that's your answer." He kicked something on the floor. I didn't even see what it was. I didn't care. I was heading for the door.

"Listen," I opened the theatre door. "I'll call Heather,

ask her to cover. She knows the show inside and out, as much as I do."

"Watch I don't replace you with her Connor and watch that attitude."

I didn't hear the last thing he said, I was out of the door and hailing a taxi from the side of the road. The last thing I needed was to explain to my wife that my work had taken priority over our daughter's health. That would not go down well in a million years.

*****

The taxi weaved through the streets of London, passing by crowds of punters enjoying a night out. It may have been closing in to midnight, but that wasn't going to stop people from partying on a school night. I'd zoned out by the time the car pulled up to my apartment building, thinking about the show and what else had to be done before opening night.

"Here you are, mate." The driver lent his left arm on the headrest of the seat next to him and tapped the window that displayed how much I owed him.

I didn't argue with the impatient tapping. I just held my phone up to the contactless pad and paid the man.

"Thanks pal."

I closed the car door and looked up at the building we called home. The lights were still on in our apartment, which only meant two things.

Number one, Monica had fallen asleep in front of the telly again or two, Katie-May was refusing to go to sleep and Monica was rocking her back and forth to make her sleepy.

Quietly opening the front door to our two-bedroom apartment, I peered inside before announcing my presence. My wife, hand on hip, was staring back at me with fire in her eyes and a raised eyebrow. One foot tapped on the laminate floor.

"Where the hell have you been?" She 'anger' whispered at me. "I know you love your job, but getting home at this hour? Is that bloody director making you stay? late again? Because I will march my ass in there and tell him he can't expect you to stay up late every night!"

Monica's rants are always amusing, and I always find it hard not to laugh every time. Instead of ordering another round of abuse I dropped my backpack which landed with a thump, there goes my laptop with all the tech queues on, and pulled her into a hug. Dismissing all the anger and annoyance she had stored up over the evening.

"I'm sorry Monica. I promise it won't always be like this." I pull back to make sure the fire in her eyes has been extinguished and stroke a piece of hair out of her eyes. "As soon as the show opens, Sean won't be needed and we can find a pattern that fits everyone's home life."

"Promise?" She looked up at me. The fire had gone, but it was still simmering. "Because I distinctly remember the last show you did, you were working late into the night."

I let out a long sigh and collapsed on the sofa. Here comes the same argument we always have.

"Not this again Monica."

"Yes, this again." She stood in front of me, hand on his, again. "It was fine before, working late, but now we have a daughter who we both need to care for."

"I'm taking Katie to the surgery tomorrow!"

"I know." She turned on her heel, facing away from me. "But what about the other times? When I need you to be there when I can't," she sniffed. "When I can't_"

Tears? Tears and sniffing? She's not telling me something.

Standing up, I rub her arms. "What's wrong Monica? What aren't you telling me?" She lets out this long sigh, like I'm supposed to already know. "Have I done something? Please, tell me so I can make it right."

"It's not you Connor."

LIES!

She leans her head on my chest. "I'm sorry, I shouldn't have gone off at you like that."

"Then what is it?"

"I'm finding it hard. Taking care of Katie whilst running a household, working from home and trying to be a good wife. It's just all a bit too much for one person to do." She turns to look at me. "That's all."

Turning her around to face the door that led to our bedroom, I marched her forward. "What you need to do is sleep. I've got tomorrow morning covered and if it helps you to relax, I'll even take Katie to the theatre tomorrow." I sat her down on the bed. Bending down, I removed her slippers and pulled the duvet back. "Have you 'you' day. Take the day off. Watch some crap on Netflix. I don't want you to feel any more stressed than you already are."

Leaning into the memory foam pillow, Monica pulled me down to sit with her on the side of the bed. "Really? You mean it?"

I kissed her forehead. "I mean it. Now. You sleep," I threw the duvet back over her body. "I'm just gonna wash and I'll be in within minutes."

*****

Did I sleep? Did I hell. Monica, on the other hand, slept all night. The promise that I would take care of Katie for the day must have been exactly what she needed to hear to pass out. Now, I had to deliver that promise. Taking my daughter to the doctors, not an issue. Taking her to work with me? To a theatre? Where we had to remain silent during rehearsals? Not my best moment. That was probably my own exhaustion speaking, but I couldn't back out of it now.

Sitting up in bed, I stole a glance at my sleeping wife. A small, but very much there, puddle of drool had soaked her pillow. The joys of wearing plastic retainers! But, hey! If you want to keep those teeth straight after paying out a fortune for braces, the needs must. I gently lifted her enough to turn the pillow. For the past two years of her wearing the retainers, she still has no idea that I have witnessed the drool factor, and I intend to keep it that way. I know she would die of embarrassment if she knew I saw that every morning, not that I care. She's still as beautiful as the day I met her. Drool and all!

As if on queue I hear grumbles from the baby monitor. The other lady in my life was awake. Reluctantly removing my tired body from the comforts of our bed, I slipped into some joggers and opened Katie's bedroom door. There she was. Standing up and holding onto the edges of her crib. How she could stand already was insane! She'd be running rings around the pair of us before we even said 'No, Katie-May, not the telly!'. I picked her up.

"Good morning, beautiful." I kissed her blonde head. Her hair doing a mighty fine impression of a mohawk. "Did you have sweet dreams?" I propped her on my hip, picked up Miss Pudding Head, yes she had a random purple and quite terrifying furry looking thing we call Miss Purple Head, and made my way to make her breakfast. A task that will in no doubt cover me in baby food and milk. However, first things first. On goes the state-of-the-art coffee machine my mother-in-law bought us for our wedding anniversary. Needs must! I sat Katie in her high chair and went about showing her every baby food jar until she decided on the flavour for the morning. She squealed when I presented her with a rhubarb and banana smoothie. Preparing myself with a tea towel, and making my coffee, I readied myself for the mess when my phone buzzed across the kitchen table. The name? Sean.

"No Sean, not this morning." I ignored the buzzing until it stopped. "Ok peanut, open for Daddy, here comes the plane." I moved the spoon side to side, making aeroplane sounds. I was millimetres away from the first mouthful, this was going to be the cleanest breakfast, ever when... BUZZ. Sean, again! Dropping the spoon back in the jar, and royally pissing my daughter off who was staring at her breakfast in disappointment, I pressed the speakerphone.

"What, Sean?"

"We are still on for an early start?"

Fuck's sake! This twat waffle doesn't listen.

Returning to my duties as 'Dad', I picked up the spoon, giving Katie a mouthful of bananas and rhubarb.

"I thought I made myself very clear last night, Sean. I won't be in until later this afternoon because my daughter comes first today." Sean let out an over dramatic groan. I got in there again before the theatrics were unleashed. "I called Heather and she is more than happy to step into my shoes until I get there later, so please, for the love of God, will you get the hint! I'm not coming in."

Hanging up on the twit felt good. Too good. There was no doubt I'd be paying for it later, but right now, I did not care. I had other priorities to take care of and a below average show with a diva for the lead and an anxiety filled director was not it.

I was jolted out of my haze by Katie. Her tiny hands slammed down on her high chair table and let out a scream that was sure to wake Monica. Great!

"Ok, ok, I'm sorry." I offered her the spoon once more. "Here you go, madam."

She happily accepted the spoon, enjoying the mushy disguising slop, that is baby food, and went to town on getting it all over her face. Bath time before the doctors then. One breakfast down, and one coffee already drunk, I made sure Katie was clean and ready before gently waking my wife. I couldn't quite believe it. She was still fast asleep, despite my daughter attempting to wake the entire building.

"Monica?" I stroked her hair. "You awake, babe?"

"Hmmm?"

"Just checking you're ok. I'm about to shower. Katie is in the crib next to you. She's fine. I'll literally be five minutes."

Rule number, fuck knows, make showing as quick as humanly possible when you have a child.

Monica stretched and let out a long yawn. The way she scrunched up her face and raised her arms wouldn't usually be attractive to anyone, but I thought it was adorable.

"Yeah, I'm awake." She turned toward where Katie's crib was and opened one eye to monitor her.

Hot! I am a lucky man!

Within less than five minutes, I had brushed my teeth, showered and styled my hair. That is a personal record. Throwing on a fresh set of black, I tied my steel toe capped boots laces and planted a kiss on Monica's head.

"Be back later. Have a relaxed day off and call me if

you need anything, ok?"

"Sure."

"We'll be fine."

I was about to close the bedroom door, to allow her to get some more sleep, when it swung open.

"Connor?" Monica stood there, hair a mess and yesterday's mascara smudge under her eyes. "Thank you." She threw her arms around me and Katie. "You have no idea how much I need this." Holding her breath, dramatically to make a point, she gave me a peek on the lips. "Love you."

"Love you too, babe."

CHAPTER TWO

It's official. I am the worst father ever. The way Katie is looking at me, I can feel the anger coming through her glare. She hates me, and I don't blame me. If anyone were to come at me with a syringe, I would probably hate them too. Two stickers later, claiming Katie was a brave girl and another for me saying I'm a good Dad, we were off to the theatre.

Yay! What joys will await me today. At least I know my crew will be happy to see this bundle of grumpiness. One capote of Heather and I will be a forgotten Father.

I should explain. Heather is a friend from way back when and Monica loves her like a sister. Any show I'm involved in, Heather, is at my right-hand side. Now, I know what people think.

'Are Conner and Heather having an affair? How could he do that to his wife?'

Well, you could not be more wrong. Heather and I are old university friends, and that is as far as it ever got. Also, as far as either of us wanted to go. We never had feelings for one another. She's my best friend. She was my best man/woman at our wedding, and she is also Katie's godmother. She's family. So now, I'm not sleeping with Heather. With no offence to her; yuck! Some things are just wrong on all accounts. And, yes, she would think the same as me.

Instead of using the main entrance, I opted for the stage door. That way I could sneak in quietly, in a hope that no one would notice me and start making demands. Luckily, the cast were in the middle of the scene so everyone's focus was on them. Making my way backstage with Katie, who was now transfixed with the lights high above her, I stationed myself next to Heather, who was barking orders through the cans.

"Lighting queue thirty? Stand by." She turned the script, following my scribbled notes of when the sound and lighting should change. "Go!"

She hadn't noticed me until Katie reached to tug her hair. She was too transfixed to the job at hand. She spun, expecting to find an actor, or Sean, but when she saw Katie, her eyes lit up.

"Hey gorgeous!" She pinched her cheeks. "Are you following in your dad's footsteps? Are you gonna tell directors to fu_ what?"

Before my best friend could teach my daughter bad language, which I'm sure she already has filed away in her little mind already, someone was obviously asking Heather something over the cans.

"What are you doing Sean? You need to keep all questions until after the run. I can't respond to that now. Oh, shit." Heather paid her attention back to the script, "Sound? Queue twenty, go!" She let out a long groan. "How'd you do it Connor? How have you not punched Sean already?"

"Years of practice Heath." I point to her headset. "You want me to take over?"

She looked at me like I'd just insulted her. "I got it." "Ok." I let the work roll off my tongue. "What's with the attitude?"

"As if you don't know." The scene was long, so there wouldn't be any changes the crew had to worry about for at least seven more pages of dialogue.

"Kirina dropped, yet another vase. One of the cast quit after last night and the costume for the understudy is too big, which means we have to get it altered before opening night. Sean is pissing me off, and he hasn't stopped bitching about you all morning." She turned to look at the script, just in case another command hadn't come up unannounced. "You know I love the theatre Connor, but after this show? I'm not sure I can carry on."

Katie reached for Heather, knowing she was upset and wanted to comfort her godmother. "Gahh, mmm, baab."

"Katie makes a good point." I say, nodding along. "Telling Sean he can shove this show up his arse after opening week sounds like a tempting offer."

Now I know I said nothing would ever happen between me and Heather, but I love to see her smile and the smile she's wearing now fills me with happiness. I don't enjoy seeing my friends pissed off.

"Katie," Heather stroked her hair. "You are absolutely right, as always." She opened the channel on her headset. "Lighting? You ready for queue thirty one?"

Watching her control the crew, I felt proud. Heather had come a long way from the days when she would be assigned the assistant wardrobe offer. She had ambition to be the boss, and from what I was witnessing, there was no doubt she was there already. Hell, I may even step down now and let her run the show. Would make more time for my family. Scratching the back of my neck, I found myself thinking more and more along those lines. What would life be like without the theatre constantly down my throat? To go home and see my family at a decent hour, rather than fuck knows what time a clock? Katie wiggled in my arms, almost like she was making me aware that she was still there. Lifting her up, I rested her against my chest and rocked her ever so gently until I could feel her getting heavier; drifting to sleep.

"Connor?" a very familiar voice, stage whispered, to me. "You got a minute?"

Heather was in full stage management mode, so I daren't disturb her. I would be just as annoyed if someone interrupted me during a run, so I had all the time for Blake's minute. Instead of talking side stage, I gestured to the loading bay just a few steps away behind the black curtains. Once the door was firmly closed, I placed Katie on my hip.

"What can I do for you Blake?"

Blake, my go to assistant for all things, stood opposite me. Hands shaking and a face like a slapped arse. Sean.

"What did he do?"

"It's nothing I should be letting myself get wound up about mate, it's just I had to tell you before you found out from someone else."

"Tell me what?"

Blake rubbed his forehead, letting his hand slowly pull his face down. "Sean's been talking smack about you all morning."

"So I've heard from Heather. What's new?"

"Well, it's not just that he'd been a moaning ass bitch, but he's been dropping gossip that he might fire you because,"

"Don't you dare tell me it's because of my priorities."
I pointed to Katie, who was still fast asleep and drooling
down my black top. Blake slowly nodded. "Arsehole! As if
he thinks he has the power to even try to fire me. Here,"
I passed Katie to him. He didn't mind. Everyone loved
my daughter. "I'll be back in a minute."

Typing as fast as I could to send a message to Monica
that I was about to beat the living shit out of the
director, I marched through the backstage area and into
the auditorium where I knew Sean would be sitting,
scribbling notes. I stood in the back row. The cheaper
seats. Why? Because you have to deal with the balcony
disturbing your view of the stage. I ran my hand across
each velvet seat as I crept up on Sean, quietly taking the
seat behind him. I leaned in close.

"I've been hearing some very disturbing things Sean."
I whisper directly into his ear. I may be a 'stagehand' to
this prick, but I can act as well. My parents didn't send
me to any old university. Oh no. I attended a drama
school that also specialises in stage management, and
we had to learn all the crafts. If I wanted to make myself
sound intimidating, I could. At the drop of a hat.

"To think, I had to hear about it from Heather and
Blake. If there was an issue, wouldn't it be more
professional to talk to me directly rather than go behind
my back? The man who is in control of this show? I
mean, really, is that such a good idea? Surely you know
the rules in theatre?" Sean hadn't turned around, but he
was sweating. He was scared. Good! "I'll remind you." I
threw my arm around his shoulders, just to make this
even more awkward than it already was. "Don't annoy
the backstage crew. You never know what we might do
as payback." I forcefully tap his left shoulder. "So if there
is anything you want to tell me now, Sean, I'd consider
doing so before I really lose my shit."

Sean stood up and waved at the stage. "Take a break,
people."

The faces from the cast landed directly on me. Yeah,
they also knew what was going on. You can act, control
your emotions. Play the audience, but some expressions
are pure. And theirs, right now, looked as pissed off as I
was.

For the first time that day, Sean met my gaze. "Ok Connor, yes, I was considering firing you."

"Why?"

"Because I needed you today, and you weren't committing to what's important."

I'm not going to lie, I almost punched him. Hard. Right across the cheekbone. Instead, I scrunched up my face and tried to rein it in. Out of the corner of my eye, I spotted Blake and Heather making their way over to us and Kirina having a diva stop, also making her way over to us on the other side of the auditorium.

Sean continued. "Heather was doing an 'ok' job, but she's not you."

Error 101. Take back the comment. Heather fit brewing.

"WHAT DO YOU MEAN, I'M DOING AN 'OK' JOB!" Heather quoted "ok," with her hands, then placed both on her hips, staring Sean down. "Am I not as good as Connor? It's not like we didn't attend the same classes in uni. Arsehole!"

Blake handed Katie back to me. She was frowning, just as his production was. She babbled something that sounded like she was giving Sean the bollocking of his life. I never felt more proud.
"That's my girl."

"I'm not saying you're not as good as Connor, Heather."

"You kinda are Sean." Kirina cut in.
It took me by surprise, the last thing I expected was to have Kirina's support. I nodded her in appreciation and mouthed 'thank you'. She tilted her head back at me, then to Heather and Blake.

"You're more than lucky to have these guys Sean, they are extremely talented at what they do, but you can't talk slap about them. They have lives outside of here, even if you don't. I mean, look at the precious face." Kirina gestured to Katie. "That is where Connor's priorities lie, and if he needs to take some of the day to look after his daughter, then that has to happen. And let me tell you this," she jabbed Sean in the chest. "You fire Connor, or any of these guys, I'll walk and so will the rest of the cast. You want that?"

"Of course I don't want that_"

"Then apologise, right now." She demanded.

Sean let out a long breath and turned to me. "Kirina's right. I apologise, Connor. I fought hand and foot to have you on this show," He gestured to Heather and Black, who were standing side by side behind me. "All of you, in fact. Your reputation precedes you, and I should be a little more grateful."

Blake scoffed. "A little? Try a lot, mate."

"Indeed." Sean caught the look my daughter was giving him. She did not like this guy. "And I'm sorry to you also, Katie. I shouldn't have acted out like that to your dad. Connor? Forgive me." I raised an eyebrow at him like I was mulling it over. "Let's all take the rest of the day off. Recharge the batteries."

No one saw that coming, but we didn't hide the fact that it was the best thing we'd heard since sliced bread. Kirina bounced back to the stage, shedding her costume as she went, probably planning what she was going to do for the rest of the day. Maybe she wasn't as much of a pain in the ass diva as I thought.

*****

Instead of hailing a taxi, Blake offered to give us a lift back home. I sat in the back with Katie wrapped in my arms, leaving the front passenger seat free for Heather. He wasn't usually the guy to drive calmly through the streets of London, but when there's a baby in the back, whose dad is holding onto her for dear life, he turned into a grandpa on a Sunday afternoon who was bird watching! He pulled up outside my apartment building.

"Did you guys wanna come in for a drink?"

"Would love to mate, but I think I'm gonna head over to Mindy's." Mindy, Blake's girlfriend of two years. "I owe her some attention."

"I know what you mean. Heather? Monica would love to see you"

At the sound of my wife's voice, Heather grinned. "Just one, then I think I'll hit the gym for a few hours before binge watching reality tv." She climbed out of the car, taking Katie so I could follow.

"Until tomorrow then, Blake." I double tapped the roof of his car. "Say hi to Mindy for us."

Monica was expecting us when I opened the front door, but instead of greeting her husband, she went straight to her best friend. I never felt more rejected.

"Love you too, babe." I joked, smiling at the women hugging the life out of each other. "Like to remind you there's a kid in the middle of that?"

"Oh, shut it you," Monica said, taking Katie in her arms without glancing at me. "I've not seen Heather for weeks."

"Three days babe, it's been three days."

"Well, it feels longer. Come and take a seat hun, and tell me what in the hell went down today." Monica tapped the seat next to her, and I was about to follow her command when I realised she was talking to Heather. The three girls sat and got to talking about the day in seconds.

I rolled my eyes and got the hint. "Suppose I'll put the kettle on then."

Filling the kettle with water and flicking it on, I produced the mugs and gathered the necessaries to make the drinks. I could hear Monica and Heather talking from within the next room. Like I said, we live in an apartment so it's easy to hear what's being discussed and the subject was of course, our work.

"I don't know what he expects from you both?" Monica's voice hit a new octave. She was clearly pissed off. "Does he think Connor will just give up his responsibilities at home? And to say that you're 'ok'. Makes my blood boil Heather, it really does. What does the rest of the crew think about it?"

"They are just as annoyed as we are. You know they've supported and followed Connor on countless shows, so if Sean thinks firing Connor will solve his problems, then he's got it wrong. Connor goes, we all go. No show."

I smiled at Heather's loyalty toward me.

"We'd follow him to the end, Monica. He's one of the best stage managers out there. Sean would shoot himself in the balls if it got out that he was even toying to cut him from the production."

"The industry can be brutal. Connor's told me that a million times."

"Exactly, and a rumour like that would ruin him as a director."

Stirring my wife's tea and placing the final mug on the tray, I grabbed a pack of chocolate digestives and joined the women in the living room.

"One coffee, with sugar and milk for Heather. White tea for my gorgeous wife and a black coffee for me." I handed the mugs out and took a seat on a large cushion on the floor. "Enjoy."

A brief silence hung as everyone enjoyed their first sip. Katie looked between us with her big eyes, probably wondering where her drink was.

"What's the plan for the rest of your day then Heather?" I ask, wiggling my butt on the cushion to make some kind of dent ass dent.

"Well, I was thinking."

"Careful." Monica teased, resulting in an elbow to the ribs from her best friend.

"You two haven't been on a date for a while, especially since this beauty arrived and the demands of the show, so I thought, if you like, I'd give you the night off."

"Heath, you don't need to do that. We have days_"

"Don't even argue with me Monica. I want to do this." Heather looked at me. "For both of you. I'll watch Katie for the night, I wouldn't be doing much else. Just watching rap on TV, anyway. Go out, enjoy yourselves."

I felt a sad smile creep up on my face. Her kindness came out of nowhere and it knocked me emotionally. "Thank you Heather, but we now owe you."

"Oh, I know. I've been saving these favours for years!"

CHAPTER THREE

A million cuddles, kisses and double checks that Katie was ok, we were finally on the way to a restaurant in Covent Garden.

I grabbed a quick shower before we left and changed into 'non theatre' clothes. It was nice to wear some colour for a change. Yeah, because I'm always in and out of theatres, there usually isn't much point in wearing anything else. I decided to sport a dark grey pair of chinos, a purple shirt and my favourite dress trainers. Yes, dress trainers, I said it. A pair of black leather slip on vans. Finishing itwith a spray of Monica's favourite cologne. If we were having a date night, then I'm pulling out all the stops. Monica, well, she looked divine. She'd slipped into a pair of tight high waisted skinny jeans, rolled up at the ankle. Sexy as fuck strappy heels. A white t-shirt, tucked into the jeans, which emphasised her small waist and finished it with a black jacket. Her golden hair draped over one shoulder. I was done. She looked hot as hell.

"Connor?" She tapped my knee.

"Huh?"

"We're here."

I glanced out of the taxi's window. "Yeah."

I paid the driver with my phone and opened the door, extending my hand for Monica out. Ok, so my mind was elsewhere during the drive. Mainly to how beautiful my wife looked and how much I wanted to take her in my arms and take her in the back of the taxi. Lacing my fingers through hers, we joined the growing public of Covent Garden. I looked around. It was early evening. That time of night when theatre goers were finishing their dinner and making their way to the theatre of choice. Covent Garden was the host too many shows. The theatres circled the borough, but it also hosted some of the best restaurants. I let out a sigh.

"What's wrong Connor?"

"It's weird." I wrapped my arm around her shoulders, wanting to feel her even closer to me. "I haven't seen this side of the theatre for years."

She followed my gaze. To the queue forming outside the Royal Opera House. "The impatient audiences?"

I let out a laugh. "I know it sounds weird, but when that is going on outside, I'm usually running rings around the cast trying to get everyone to be ready on time. It's just weird to be on this side of it for a change."

"Do you miss it?"

"What do you mean?"

"I mean, do you miss seeing this side? You know," she pulls away from me. "Not being in the theatre?"

I stare at her as zero words form in my brain to her question. Not being in the theatre. The thought of not working in the west end had never crossed my mind.

"Uh, I, I don't know." I take her hand back in mine as we near the restaurant, my mind racing with thoughts. "I've been doing this career for as long as I can remember, I don't know how I feel about stepping away from it all."

She laughs and kisses my hand. "I didn't mean you should leave. I meant just seeing what the theatre staff see each night. The audience's excitement? Their thrill of seeing live theatre? That 'after show' buzz?"

Part of me knew what she meant, but it didn't stop my brain from thinking about it. What would life be like away from the theatre? No panic when a prop is broken or when a set dress does wrong on opening night. When the sound guys fuck up and play the wrong effect. No Sean.

With the restaurant to my left, I turn to Monica. My rock. My life. The only woman I care about making happy. The absolute love of my life.

"What if I walked away from it?"

"Connor?"

"Leave theatre after this show, fuck it, maybe even sooner."

"Sweetheart, you've had a bad day. Do nothing."

"Irrational? Why not?" Swinging her around to face me, I felt a sense of relief falling over me. Like a weight has been taken off my shoulders, just toying with the idea. "What if I did? We'd have more time, more evenings. No more stupid late nights?"

"But you'd miss it. Eventually. You love this job, it's

just this show in particular that's pushing you to think like this, Connor." Monica laid her hand on my cheek and stroked the area just below my eye with her thumb. "Think it through, sweetheart. Please?"

Covering her hand with mine, I looked deep into her eyes. "Of course."

*****

The following days went by in a blur of rehearsals, last-minute adjustments and opening night preparations. For me and my crew, we were double checking everything for the evening's performance. From the feeling around throughout the theatre, the afternoon off did everyone the world of good. People's work ethics had been reset and a new level of respect had fallen upon the cast and crew. Even Sean seemed happier. Probably because I roasted his ass for being a twat. This new feeling hasn't stopped my mind from thinking what life would be like away from live theatre, though. It was still in the forefront of my mind. Monica was right, I should think about it. What would I do if I left? Would I still want to work in the industry? I certainly can't see myself working in an office. Pen pushing and typing figures into pointless spreadsheets for someone to look at then delete. Lucky for me, being good at my job, I had contacts. Contacts as television and film. During a break, I snuck out the stage door and opened my phone. I checked no one was nearby before I pressed 'call'. I'm not sure if it was my excitement of a career change or the first night nerves, but I couldn't stop my hands from shaking.

"Connor, my man." Eddie, another friend from university, answered the call. He was always happy. There had never been a day in our friendship that I saw him angry. "How's tricks, mate?"

"Hey Ed. Sorry to call during what I imagine is a busy day for you."

"Never too busy for you Con, you know that. What's up?"

I let out a long sigh, and double checked no one was behind me again. Knowing my luck of this production, someone had a recording device to capture my call. "Remember, you said if I needed a break,"

"Of course."

"Well," I groaned. "Theatre life. You know how it is."

"You need a change, don't you?"

"Yeah. This show is the last nail in the coffin Ed and it's not just the drama that goes with it. I have to make a change, for Monica and Katie."

Ed grunted. "I get you Connor. I really do. Leaving the theatre was the best thing I could have done for my family."

"Really?"

"Sure, I still work the occasional late night, but not every night. Listen, I know what you're going through and I've got you, mate."

"You have no idea how much I appreciate this Ed."

"Finish this run and I'll talk with the station manager, who has become a close friend. You're a talent in your own right Connor and anyone would be daft not to pick you up."

"Thanks Ed."

"Leave it with me and I'll get back to you. Stay strong mate."

Ed hung up and for the first time since I started on this show, I could see the light at the end of a long tunnel. A means to an end. An end to the stress and sleepless nights. I could see my family spending more time together and although I may secretly miss the buzz of live theatre, I had to do what was right for my family, and if stepping away from a career that I thought would lead me into retirement, then that was exactly what I had to do.

I want to be happy, and being in a position where I found myself counting down the hours was not it.

THE END

Thank you for reading my short stories.
These novellas featured alongside some incredible authors in the box sets listed below.

Miracle At Midnight - SECRET SANTA (USA Today Bestseller)

Selfridges - HOLLY JOLLY

Arguing whether the answer is 8 or 10 - LOVE IN THE DUMPSTER FIRE

Stand By Me - FALLING FOR LOVE

About The Author

Long and short of it, I am a published author.

An urban contemporary romance author, as I like to put it, and I have been writing for over six years.

Growing up, I was very much into theatre and I have graced the stage more than a few times, but over the years, I discovered the joy in creating worlds of my own, but what began as a hobby, soon grew into a passion.

Writing is like escapism for me and my overactive imagination. When I was a kid, my teachers used to call me a daydreamer, and on multiple occasions tell me to pay attention. (They put it down to my lack of ability, but I actually grew up with hearing problems.)

Well, call me a daydreamer all you want, but that imagination has got me to where I am today. So, thank you.

Beckinsale was born in Somerset, England, to parents who were in The Royal Navy. She has two elder brothers, who she looked up to as she grew and still does. It was her brother, Philip, who encouraged her to perform. She still lives in Somerset with her husband, Geraint.

Amy was always quiet when she was young, keeping her thoughts to herself. Many thought she was shy, but things changed and now she gets excited to share her work with the world. She has always been a dreamer and believes it is what has got her to where she is today.

"Dreams and ambitions drive us to where we want to be. You wouldn't be imagining that life, if it weren't to be."

Stalk Amy Online

Read More of Author's Books

Printed in Great Britain
by Amazon